Manual A. Fuentes

Lima

Sketches of the capital of Peru, historical statistical, administrative, commercial and

moral

Manual A. Fuentes

Lima
Sketches of the capital of Peru, historical statistical, administrative, commercial and moral

ISBN/EAN: 9783337383008

Printed in Europe, USA, Canada, Australia, Japan

Cover: Foto ©Andreas Hilbeck / pixelio.de

More available books at **www.hansebooks.com**

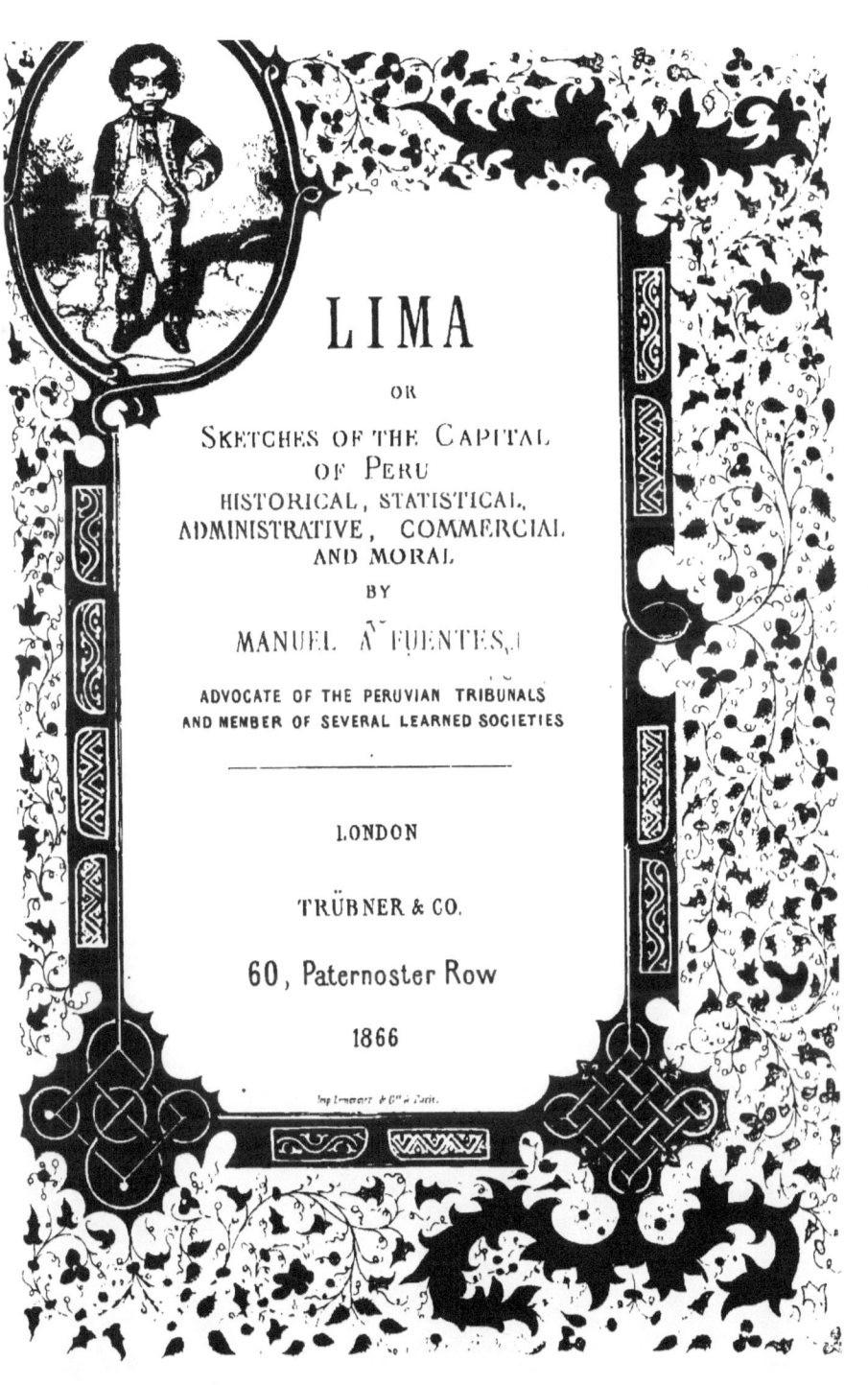

LIMA

OR

SKETCHES OF THE CAPITAL
OF PERU
HISTORICAL, STATISTICAL,
ADMINISTRATIVE, COMMERCIAL
AND MORAL

BY

MANUEL A. FUENTES,

ADVOCATE OF THE PERUVIAN TRIBUNALS
AND MEMBER OF SEVERAL LEARNED SOCIETIES

LONDON

TRÜBNER & CO.

60, Paternoster Row

1866

Imp. Lemercier & Cⁱᵉ à Paris.

To

my daughter

PARIS 1867

Imp. Lemercier & Cie, 57 rue de Seine, à Paris

At a moment when the attention of all Europe has been turned towards Peru by the recent proceedings of the Spanish squadron in the Pacific Ocean, we flatter ourselves that the following *Sketches* of LIMA, the capital of that republic, will be received with favour by the reading world.

The manners and customs of that fairyland, whose very name has become a proverb, have been constantly misrepresented by the narratives of fantastic voyagers, who, being thoroughly ignorant of the country, have mistaken mere accidental circumstances for the general characteristics of its inhabitants. Many of these writers, indeed, seem to belong to the same category as the French traveller, who, having happened, on arriving at Madrid one day about noon, to see two desperate fellows fighting with long knives, at once noted down in his pocket-book that such was the constant habit of Spaniards every day about that hour. Or the Englishman, who, on issuing one evening from a railway terminus in Paris, and seeing a hackney-coach knock down and run over an elderly lady, instantly drew the inference that the Parisians made a practice of thus crushing all old women who ventured out into the streets after dusk.

Statements as absurd as these have often been made by tourists who thought their remarks deserved the honour of publication. If men can be found to talk so idly of neighbouring nations, whose manners differ but little from their own, what may not be expected from persons of the same calibre who visit distant parts of the world where far greater differences exist, as in South America, for instance?

Europe in general is most imperfectly acquainted with the people of these remote regions, only studying them in a commercial point of view; in other respects, their political condition, their usages, and their civilization, are judged in the most superficial manner, without due reflection, and in most cases, with unjust temerity.

We are by no means disposed, from an excess of patriotism, to fall into the opposite absurdity, by asserting that the American States have attained the high level of the Old World. Not long since freed from the yoke of colonization, placed under circumstances and conditions anything but favourable for rapidly raising them to the rank of independent nations, they have had, and still have, to struggle against the horrors of anarchy.

However, in the midst of continual civil wars, which force the husbandman and artisan from their homes to engage in a fratricidal combat, civilization has made incredible advances in the short period of forty-two years.

The rare intervals of *repose* which Peru has enjoyed (we say *repose*, because the restless spirit of aspirants to power has never permitted the country to be really at peace) have

sufficed to sweep away those old customs which might serve
as a subject for the satire of our enemies and calumniators.

The society of Lima has no reason to envy that of the
most civilized capitals: there are even European nations in
which woman, the inestimable helpmate of man, the soul
and the consolation of the domestic hearth, is far from offering all the charms of the fair Limanian. Cheerfulness,
talent, beauty, amiability—in short, all the physical, intellectual, and moral qualities which make woman the most precious jewel of the earth—all these gifts, we repeat, have
been bountifully lavished, by the hand of God, on the Limanian women. Has it not often been said of the ladies of
Lima that they have the eyes and looks of the Italian, the
perfect figure and gracefulness of the French, and the wit of
the Andalusian?

There is no exaggeration in what we have here said. As to
their personal appearance, the reader may form some idea
from the engravings accompanying these sketches, which are
accurate copies of photographs, due to the pencils of the
best artists of Paris. They are faithful reproductions of nature's handiworks.

The travellers from different countries, who, of late years,
have written about Peru, seem to have had in view what
might have existed before the Conquest. At the present moment, a collection of voyages is in course of publication at
Paris. If we may judge of the accuracy of the accounts concerning other nations of the world by the articles on Peru
contained in this work, it would seem as if the authors had
no other object than to write a romance in which all the characters described are of the most savage type.

One of our most venerable priests (1), an indefatigable la-
bourer in the work of civilizing the native tribes, was not
indeed a model of manly beauty, but he nevertheless had a
pleasing exterior, with an intelligent and modest air. Well!
in the work above-mentioned, this gentleman is represented
with the vulgar aspect of a muleteer (2).

In the same collection, we also find among other types, all
of the most fanciful kind, a seminarist of Cuzco, and an
Indian *rabona* (3). The former has the appearance of a bee-
hive surmounted by a mask with a broad-brimmed hat on it;

(1) The Reverend Father Plaza.
(2) We give an exact copy of the engraving in question, which is stated to be a
faithful portrait of Father Plaza.
(3) Soldier's wife.

the latter looks like a Fury, with a Medusa's head, carrying not only her kitchen utensils, but also the complete appointments of a soldier. We really cannot imagine what induces travellers to draw upon fancy for the materials of their books, instead of depicting what they must have seen. If they meet with any uncouth or deformed individual, why should they present him or her as the type of a family, a race, or a corporation?

A veracious writer only introduces such persons, as he does humorous anecdotes, to enliven his narrative, but, to set them forth as representatives of a country, is not only offering an affront to that country, but also injurious to his own reputation as a traveller or historian. As for ourselves, in our sketches of manners and customs, we portray them as they have been and also as they are at present. Our object is to give a summary account of our political organization; to prove that in our establishments of public instruction and charity, the departments which best show the civilization of a country, we have made as much progress as we could; that foreign trade is extending on a large scale, and finds abundant support in the free expenditure of the wealthy; that the manners of the people are improving, in proportion as the practices introduced by bad taste and barbarism disappear; and, lastly, that we do not deserve to be regarded as savage denizens of primeval forests, half-covered with feathers, who shoot down foreigners with bows and arrows and afterwards eat them raw at a family banquet.

Paris, 1806.

ADVERTISEMENT.

The literary and descriptive sketches are extracted from the *Statistics of Lima* and the *Traveller's Guide*. The latter has also supplied some few articles on popular customs. The author trusts that his readers will excuse him for thus borrowing from his own works.

LIMA.

PART I.

FOUNDATION AND DESCRIPTION OF LIMA.

THE city which is now the capital of Peru was founded by the Conqueror, Francisco Pizarro, on the 18th of January 1535 under the name of *Ciudad de los Reyes* (City of the Kings).

The capital of the old viceroyalty was the town of Jauja, the principal inhabitants of which joined with the municipality and the *justicias* (judicial and administrative authorities) in representing to Pizarro how unsuitable that place was to remain the seat of government.

Pizarro appointed commissioners to explore the valley of Pachacamac in the district of the cacique of Lima, and as they reported that the territory bathed by the Rimac was well adapted, owing to its proximity to the sea and other advantages, to become the site of the capital, he decreed, at the date above mentioned, that the city should be founded there.

Form and Extent of Lima. — The configuration of the city is irregular, something in the shape of a triangle, whose base, or longest side, rests on the river, which divides it into two parts, the

View from the *Arrabal de San Lazaro.*

upper, and the lower; the latter was formerly called the *Arrabal* (suburb) *de San Lázaro.*

View of Lima, taken from the *Arco del Puente.*

The whole city is two-thirds of a league in length, and its greatest width two-fifths of a league.

The original extent of Lima was twenty-two cuadras (1) from east to west, fourteen from north to south. Its present area is 13,343,680 square Castilian varas, of which 2,438,000 are occupied by gardens and *muladares* (rubbish-shoots) in the upper part; and 2,412,320 by gardens, in the lower part; 126,150 by squares; 674,552 by churches and convents; leaving 7,692,658 for dwellings. The whole of the lower part is surrounded by strong walls built in 1683, during the viceroyalty of the Duke of La Palata.

Geographical and Topographical Position. — The city is situated in 12° 2′ 34″ south latitude, and in 70° 55′ 20″ west longitude from the meridian of Cadiz; 77° 7′ 36″ from Greenwich, and 79° 27′ 45″ from Paris.

Lima is exposed to winds from the south and west, but sheltered by the mountains on the north and east.

These mountains are spurs of the great chain of the Andes, which runs nearly north and south twenty leagues to the east of the capital. The eastern spurs descend gradually from north to south forming deep valleys. Those of the north accompany from east to west the right bank of the Rimac, at a greater or less distance. Opposite the higher part of Lima, they make a sweep, touching the commencement of the *arrabal* of San Lázaro with the skirts of Mount San Cristobal, at the foot of which the Rimac enters the city. The summits of San Cristobal and of Amancaes are the highest of all these ridges; the former being 470 Castilian varas, and the latter 960, above the level of the sea.

Westward the city commands a view of the Pacific about two leagues distant; in the south-west, the island of San Lorenzo is visible; and in the south the *Morro Solar* or *Morro of Chorrillos*. On the south rise a number of sand hills, running eastward,

(1) The length of the *cuadra* (front of a block of houses) was from 120 to 140 Spanish varas or yards, equal to 2 feet 9 inches English. The vara is divided into three feet, each of which is consequently 11 English inches. The square vara contains 7.56 square feet, or about five-sixths of the English square yard.

and gradually increasing in size till they join the Cordilleras.

Nature of the Soil. — Several strata of sand and pebbles lie between the surface and the solid rock, which is always found at a certain depth. This structure of the soil, resembling that of the bottom of the sea off the coast, seems to indicate that at some period the ocean covered two or three leagues beyond the shore it now bathes. The shells found, both north and south, scattered over the hills, themselves formed of sand and marine detritus, as well as many other indications, justify the conclusion that, not many centuries back, the sea covered those enormous masses of granite which form the last ramifications of the Cordilleras.

Seasons. — It may truly be stated that only two distinct seasons are known at Lima — winter and summer. Though neither the heat nor the cold is so intense as in some other countries, both have considerable power. Spring, summer, autumn, and winter respectively begin towards the end of September, December, March, and June. The dog-days last from the 23rd of January to the 8th of March.

Winds. — The south wind prevails on the coast; the north blows at intervals, according to the hour of the day and the season of the year. At sunrise there is generally a light breeze from the west, veering round to the south about noon. The northerly wind felt at Lima comes from the north-west, owing to the direction of the chain of mountains in the vicinity : it sets in between one and two in the morning and continues for about eight hours.

The daily movement of the winds is always against the sun.

Rain. — Lima never has any of those continous rains which are common in the mountainous districts farther inland and in some countries of Europe. Towards the end of April or the beginning of May, the *garuas* (1) set in, and continue till November with more or less intermission. During the rest of the year, they only occur at the changes of the moon.

In summer, rain often falls, but in heavy showers of very short duration.

---

(1) *Garuas*, very small rain, like what is called a *Scotch mist*.

Earthquakes. — Lima is exposed to strong shocks, which have more than once left it a heap of ruins. These phenomena occur most frequently between spring and summer, but are not altogether unknown in autumn. The shocks usually pass from south to north, following the direction of the chain of mountains. Among the earthquakes which have caused the greatest ravages may be especially mentioned those of 1630, 1687, 1746, 1806, and 1828. On an average there are eight in a year.

Streets. — The thoroughfares of Lima are well laid out, and present a pleasing aspect to the eye; some of them, however, are disfigured by open sewers, by a want of uniformity in the exterior of

View of the *Calle de las Mantas* (now *de Callao*).

the edifices, and by the system of Moorish balconies which was introduced by the Spaniards. Though most of the wooden lattices which used to give these balconies the appearance of bird-cages have recently been replaced by glazed windows, the unequal height of their heavy masses, projecting at least three feet from the wall, assuredly does not contribute to the beauty of the streets.

Pizarro, on planning the city, assigned lots of building-ground to the first founders, who, on account of their limited number, built only three short streets, the first being that which runs by the side of the cathedral, called *Calle de los Judíos* (Jew-street).

There are now three hundred and fifty-six of these streets, exclusive of thoroughfares which have been laid out, but as yet have no buildings in them. The streets do not run in the direction of the four cardinal points, but they are quite straight and intersect each other at right angles; forming square blocks of houses called *manzanas*. The length of the streets is from 120 to 140 varas, some varying a little both in length and width.

View of the *Calle del Teatro* (now *Huancavelica*).

Each *cuadra* (front) of these blocks contains from twenty to thirty doorways belonging to large dwelling-houses or shops. The regularity of the streets and the great number of towers scattered about the capital render it a very fine sight from the neighbouring heights, though the shape of the roofs somewhat detracts from its beauty; as the very slight rainfall prevents the necessity for tiled angular roofs, the tops of the houses are all quite flat.

Imp. Jouaust, r. du Croissant, 16, Paris

Some few years ago each *cuadra* in Lima had a distinct name of its own, and it is interesting to note the origin of some of them such as *Borricos, Pericotes, Ya Parió, Patos,* etc. (1)

At the present day, though the different cuadras standing in the same straight line have only name, it may fairly be said that the municipality has not shown much tact in approving of the designation selected; all are names of provincial capitals or towns, and many of them are words of the purest *Quichua* (2), which foreigners, the English especially, can never pronounce.

Houses. — The houses of Lima have a cheerful appearance seldom found in those of other countries. Internally, they are in general extremely convenient, and for decoration, cleanliness, ele-

View of the Hotel del Universo.

gance, and even sumptuousness, they are in no way inferior to those of the most civilized countries. The same praise cannot, however, be given to their fronts, which, being constructed in defiance of all the rules of architecture, unequal in height, and fan-

(1) *Borricos,* donkeys; *Pericotes,* mice; *Ya Parió,* she has just been delivered; *Patos,* ducks.

(2) *Quichua,* the primitive Indian language.

tastically painted, are far from corresponding to the taste which characterizes the inhabitant of Lima.

The houses are by no means lofty. The majority have two stories,
but a few have three; the fear of earthquakes has hitherto deterred
from erecting higher buildings. However, this timidity has begun
to disappear, since skilful architects have adopted the precaution
of giving their structures greater stability by the judicious combi-
nation of iron and stone.

In the year 1793 the total number of outer doors in Lima was
8,222, in 3,641 houses; in 1847, there were 13,093; in 1860,
14,002; in 1864, 14,209.

In 1860, the doors were thus divided: 164 belonged to public
establishments, including colleges and hospitals; 3,003 to large
mansions; 2,621 to middle-sized and small houses; 471 to *callejo-
nes de cuartos* (lodgings for operatives); 5,742 to shops and ware-
houses; 499 to coach-houses; 326 to *altillos* (first–floor apartments
approached by outside stairs); 92 to stables and yards; 318 *puertas
falsas* (back-doors for servants); and 166 walled-up doors; this last
number is yearly decreasing on account of new buildings being
erected.

Town-gates. — The upper part of Lima, as already stated, is
enclosed by walls, in which there are twelve gates: the Callao,
San Jacinto, Martinete, Maravillas, Barbones, Cocharcas, Santa Catalina, two Guadalupes, Juan Simon, and two Monserrats. The
lower part, completely encircled by the mountains, has two en-
trances, Guia, and La Piedra Liza.

The best-built and handsomest of these gates are the Callao and
Maravillas : the former leads from the city to a spacious public
walk planted with trees, which, as well as the gateway itself, was
executed under the Viceroy O'Hinggins in 1797, the necessary funds,
amounting to 343,000 piastrés, having been supplied by the Consulado (Tribunal of Commerce) of Lima. The front was very beautiful; over the middle door, which is the largest, were placed the
royal arms with the inscription, *Imperante Carolo IV;* over the
right-hand one, the arms of Lima, and over the left those of the

Front of the old palace

of the Marquis de Torre Tagle

Fot. de Courret Hermanos   Paris Imp Godard r du Jardinet 27

Consulado. All these escutcheons, and the ornaments on which they rested, were removed some years since, and a plain cornice is now the only ornament of the gateway.

Squares and Public Places. — Of these there are thirty-three in the city, all of which, with the exception of the *Plaza Mayor*, the *Independencia*, and the *Siete de Setiembre* (Seventh of September), lie round the churches whose names they bear.

The only one which, for its extent, deserves the name of a square, is the *Plaza Mayor*, in the centre of the city, which occupies an area of about a *fanegada* (nine English acres). The south-west and north-west sides are ornamented with stone columns and arcades, which form noble porticos. These were erected in 1693 in pursuance of a decree of the Viceroy Count de Monclova. The south-west portico is called the *Botoneros*, owing to the privilege granted, many years ago and recently renewed, to the trimming-makers to establish workshops there. The other side is called the *Portal de Escribanos* (notaries), because in former times *those ravens had established their nests* on that spot.

The shops under these arcades offer all the creations of European fashion in as great abundance as the most elegant and capricious of ladies can desire.

Opposite the *Portal de Escribanos* is the magnificent façade of the cathedral; and facing that of the *Botoneros* stands the edifice called the Palace of the Government.

The municipality has its offices and archives in the upper story at one extremity of the *Portal de Escribanos*.

Rivers. — The only water-course which crosses the capital, dividing it into two parts, is the Rimac, whose stream, though highest in summer, is nevertheless too scanty to water the valley through which it flows. Its course is from north-east to south-west.

To facilitate communications between the two parts of the city, a wooden bridge was built across the Rimac in 1554, which was replaced by the present stone bridge in 1610, during the viceroyalty of the Marquis of Montes Claros. It is five hundred geometrical feet in length, and consists of six arches having an elevation of one hundred and ninety feet. The whole structure is of hewn stone. At the southern part of the bridge rises a fine arch thirty cubits high. Two turrets adorn its summit, one on each side, and between them formerly stood a statue of Philip V., which was thrown down by an earthquake in 1746. On the pedestal of this statue an alle-

View of the Bridge of Lima.

gorical figure of Time has since been erected, and in a niche, which, before the earthquake, was occupied by an image of the Virgin of Belen (Bethlehem), there is now a handsome clock with two transparent dials.

The inhabitants of the lower part of the town having suffered greatly from inundations, the authorities determined, in 1637, to prevent such disasters in future by erecting large dikes of masonry, to which purpose fifty thousand piastres were devoted.

Water. — The water of the river, public fountains, and private wells contains a great quantity of calcareous salts especially sulphate of lime, but, on the whole, is pure and wholesome.

Fountains. — Before a company was established in Lima to supply houses with water conveyed through iron pipes, there were

Riviere del   Imp Godard Paris

Fountain of the Plaza Mayor of Lima

61 fountains in the city: 27 public ones, large and small; 19 in
convents and monasteries; 6 in hospitals and charitable establishments; 19 in colleges and other public institutions. There
were also 177 wells on private premises. The number of public
fountains has not been increased, but great additions have been
made to those in private houses and public establishments.

The largest fountain in the capital is the one in the Plaza Mayor.
It consists of a square stone basement, three feet and a half high,
each side measuring fifteen varas; it has stone steps all round and
an open channel to carry off the waste water. Over this basement
is the principal tazza nine varas in diameter, supported by eight
lions and as many griffins. In the centre of this rises a pedestal eighteen feet high, and composed of three parts; on this rests the second
tazza of three varas in circumference, from which water escapes
through the mouths of several masks. Above this second tazza rises
a column two feet in diameter, and two varas high, decorated with
foliage and other ornaments, with four figures holding up the third
tazza, six varas and two thirds in circumference, which receives water thrown up from ten seraphim. Another column of two varas
supports a vase of foliage which is surmounted by a statue of Fame.
The fountain is made of bronze, and its total height is fifteen varas
and one third (forty-two English feet).

At each corner of the basement, there is a basin decorated with
mouldings.

This fountain cost 85,000 piastres and was inaugurated on the
21st of September 1578.

The municipality has recently made a fine garden round the
fountain, inclosed by an iron palisade. Fountains have also been
placed in the four corners of the square, which has been well
paved, and embellished with marble vases and seats of the same
material.

Paving and Flagging. — The paving of the roadway in the
streets is the worst that can be imagined; being made of round
stones, the surface is so very uneven as to be very bad not only for
persons on foot, but also for horses and carriages. The poor animals

soon fall lame and carriages are always getting out of repair owing
to the roughness of the road. Add to this the further disadvantage
that open gutters run down many of the streets, which spread into
wide pools when any obstacle arrests their course, so as to make
walking, if not impossible, at least extremely unpleasant.

As a remedy for these inconveniences, the Government proposed to repave the streets and make sewers to carry off not only
the surface water but also the slops from the houses. As an expe-
riment a new pavement was laid down in one street and sewers
made; in two others a kind of stone tramway was laid down, -
but without under-ground drains.

The old foot pavements were as bad as the pitching; but since
1847 a new system has been introduced, and most of the streets
now have raised foot-paths about five feet wide covered with flag-
stones brought from Europe.

Lighting. — The streets are lighted with gas, in virtue of a
privilege granted by the Government to a company, which is also
bound to supply gas to all private individuals who may require it.

Population. — The first inhabitants of Lima were only seventy
in number : eleven accompanied Pizarro, thirty arrived soon after
from Sangallan, and twenty-eight joined them from Jauja. The
eleven companions of the founder were : the treasurer Alonso Ri-
quelme, the inspector Garcia de Salcedo, Nicolas de Rivera (senior),
Nicolas de Rivera (junior), Rodrigo Mazuelas, Juan Tello, Rui Diaz,
Alonso Martin de D. Benito, Cristobal Palomino, Cristobal de Peralta, and Antonio de Picado, secretary to the Government.

At present, the population amounts, according to the last cen-
sus, to 121,362 souls, of whom 26,619 are natives of Lima; 55,992
come from different parts of the Republic, and 38,761 are foreigners.

As already stated, the number of original inhabitants was seventy, including the founder; in the year 1820, according to official returns, the population was 64,000, having increased in 285
years of colonization, by 63,930 souls, and during the following
45 years of independence by 57,362. These figures show that the

average increase of population for each year of colonization was $224\frac{60}{785}$, and for each year of independence $1274\frac{14}{47}$.

The registers of births and deaths prove that, on the average, the former are 3,200 yearly, and the latter 4,000. It is necessary to observe that the deaths include many foreigners and provincials admitted into the hospitals of the city.

We shall treat, in another place, of the present population with regard to difference of race.

Public Buildings. — The first edifices erected by Pizarro were : the Cathedral, the Government Palace, the Archbishop's Palace, and the City-hall.

The *Government Palace* contains the offices and apartments of the President of the Republic, the five Ministries, or offices of the Secretaries of State; the Supreme Court of the Republic, and the chief Court of. the Department, with their secretaries' offices and archives ; the General Direction of Finance; the Court of Accounts; the General Treasury; the Stamp-office; the Staff of the Garrison, the Prefecture of the Department; the Sub-Prefecture of the Province, and the National Printing-office.

The building still retains its original form, which is certainly not the best suited for the seat of the Government of Peru. We will not attempt to describe it, as our pen shrinks from undertaking a task so unpleasant. Some few repairs and alterations have been made in the apartments of the President and in the Ministries, but they have not changed the unsightly aspect of an edifice which ought to be the best in the capital.

The palace has been occupied, from 1535 to 1821, by three governors, of whom, the Conqueror, Francisco Pizarro, was the first, and forty-three viceroys, of whom the last was D. José de Lacerna, who capitulated in 1824 with the Republican army after its victory at Ayacucho.

From 1821 to 1865, the palace has been the residence of fifty-three Chiefs of the State under different denominations, without counting five Councils of Government. The first Chief of the Republic who, under the title of *Protector of Peru*, exercised the dictatorship, was General D. J. San Martin. Of these fifty-three Chiefs of the State, only six Presidents have owed their office to popular election.

The *Archbishop's Palace,* which contains the prelate's residence, with the offices and archives of the Ecclesiastical Court, stands near the Cathedral; it presents nothing remarkable.

From 1543 down to the present time, it has been occupied by twenty-two archbishops. The first was Dr. D. F. Geronimo de Loaiza, who took possession of the bishopric of Lima in that year, and received the pallium of archbishop in 1548. The present archbishop is Senor D. D. José Sebastian de Goyeneche, the senior of all the catholic bishops now living.

Sixty-seven temples, of which one is the Cathedral, five are parish churches, two chapels of ease; six belong to convents of existing communities, two to congregations of regular clergy, thirteen to existing monasteries, four to *beaterios* (Beguin-houses); six are public chapels served by monks; thirteen are public churches or chapels; four belong to houses for religious exercises; one to nuns hospitallers, and ten to suppressed couvents.

The *Cabildo* (Municipal Council), which contains the halls for the sessions with the secretaries' offices and the archives.

The *Casa de Moneda* (Mint), with all the offices and workshops for coining. The *Tribunal of Mines* also sits in this building.

The *University,* containing the halls for literary exercices; one room in this building is occupied by the College of Advocates, and the Chamber of Deputies holds its sittings in the chapel.

The *Senate House.*

The *National Library,* part of which contains the *Museum of Antiquities* and of *Natural History.*

Eight National Colleges. — One for the study of jurisprudence; an ecclesiastical seminary; a college for the study of Medicine and the accessory sciences; one for secondary instruction; a Normal School; a Naval and Military Institute; a College for Obstetrics, and a School of Arts and Trades.

An Infant Asylum.

An Orphan School.

A Prison for accused persons.

A Penitentiary.

A Public Slaughter-house.

Five Hospitals : One for men, another for women; a third for soldiers, and two for persons affected with incurable diseases.

A Lunatic Asylum, for persons of either sex.

An *Asylum* for widows of decayed tradesmen.

A General Cemetery.

A *Consulado* (Tribunal of Commerce).

The General Administration of the Post-office and the *Direccion de Beneficencia* (Board for Relieving the Poor) have no edifices appropriated to them.

As places of amusement Lima has :

A *Theatre* (belonging to the municipality).

A *Circus for cockfighting* (private property).

A *Circus for bull-fights* (belonging to the Board for Relieving the Poor).

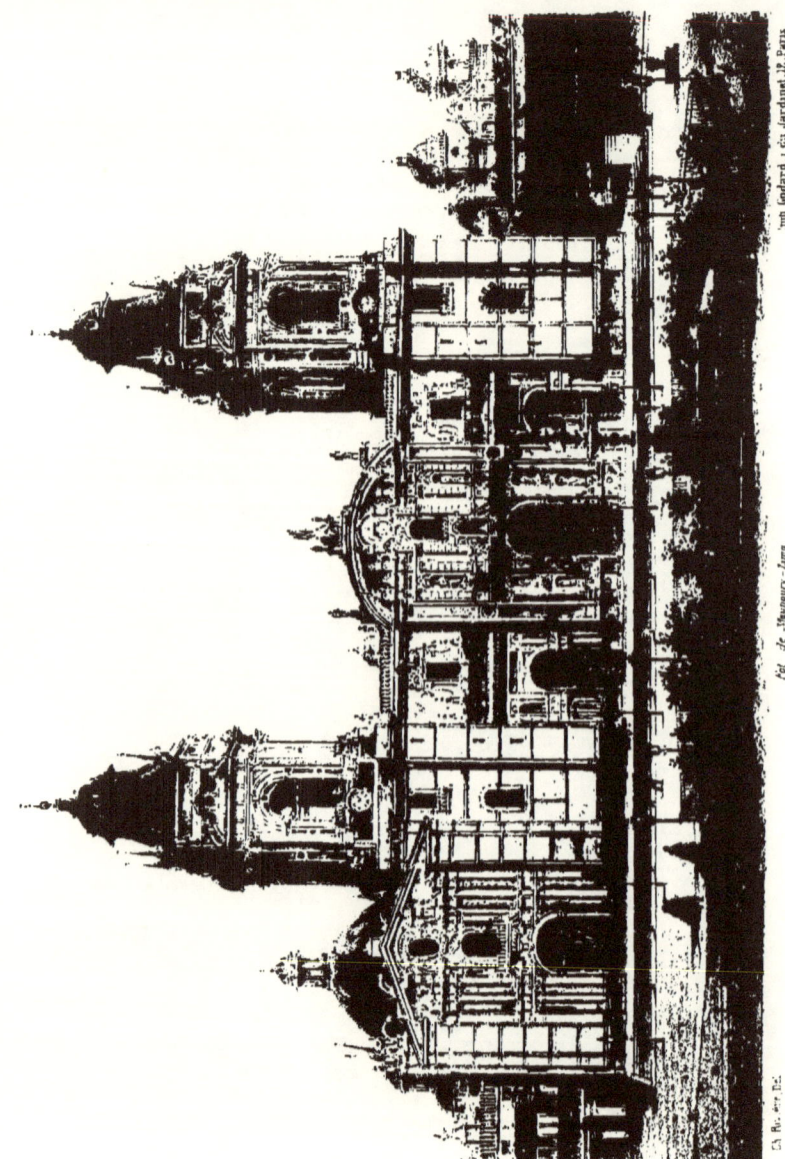

Ch. No. ere. Del.

Phot. de Neurdeins - Paris

Imp. Godard, : cu. Jardinet. 18. Paris

PART II.

PLACES OF WORSHIP.

Cathedral. — This church, as already stated, was built by Francisco Pizarro, and considerably improved by Archbishop Loaiza. Owing to earthquakes and other interruptions, it was not completed till ninety years after its foundations were laid, and its total cost was 594,000 piastres. This edifice, having been shattered by the earthquake of 1746, was rebuilt by the viceroy, Count de Superunda.

The following description taken from an old author will give an idea of the magnificence of the structure : — "The length of the front is 162 varas, including, at each end, a tower of three stories, with a square basement of the Tuscan order, uniting strength with beauty. The upper stories are faced with pilasters and have cornices so wide that the visitor, notwithstanding the great height, can walk all round outside without the least fear of falling. The towers are 55 varas high, and 14 square at the base. Each of them may be ascended by a staircase which is two varas wide at the top. The interval of 41 varas between the two towers is occupied by the three naves of the church corresponding with the doors which open towards the square, on a parvise 20 varas in width. The portals are approached by seven stone steps half a vara wide and half a foot in height, bounded at their extremities by stone parapets. An iron palisading, erected on a stone basement, and interrupted by six stone

2

pedestals supporting bronze globes, separates this parvise from the public square.

"The principal portal, the middle one, called the Door of Pardon, is five varas and a half in width, and about double that in height. It is surmounted by a most remarkable frontispiece in Panama stone, which is, beyond dispute, the finest in the kingdom. This frontispice is composed of three distinct portions : first, four fluted columns of the Corinthian order, each two feet in diameter, and high in proportion; they bear capitals of their order, architraves, and friezes decorated with sculptures in demi-relief.

Front view ot the Cathedral.

The entablatures have indentations and consoles, and on them rest pedestals serving as the basis of the second story. On each side, in the space between the columns, appear, in four lofty niches, as many statues above two varas in height, which represent the Evangelists, St. Matthew, St. Mark, and St. Luke, and lastly, that sublime doctor of the Church, St. Jerome.

"The second story, also of the Corinthian order, is composed of fluted pilasters, half a vara in depth and three-quarters wide, surmounted by Corinthian capitals with sculptured friezes and architraves. In the intervals between these pilasters are two admirably ornamented niches, containing statues of St. Peter and St. Paul.

Over the keystone of the arch of the portal, between the two principal frontispieces, in a niche of magnificent design, stands an
image of the Holy Virgin. Above this is the principal window of
the second story and in it a statue of the blessed Toribio Alfonso,
in baret, camail, and rochet, giving his blessing to an Indian kneeling before him. The third portion is a segmental pediment in
which are the royal and imperial arms, on a shield two varas wide
and three in height, surrounded by richly sculptured ornaments.

" To crown the whole, there is a pedestal bearing the statue
of St. John the Evangelist, the patron of the Cathedral, with the
eagle at his feet, the book and pen in his hands. This statue is
three varas in height.

" This splendid portal has a smaller one on each side, opening
into the lateral naves of the church. These two doors are four varas
and a half wide and eight in height. The lower part is of the Doric
order, the second and third both Corinthian. The windows above,
decorated with pilasters, arcades, friezes, cornices, and frontispieces
of Panama stone, are each nineteen varas high, being exceeded by
those of the middle portal, which are twenty-five varas.

" The church is divided into three naves and two side-aisles,
containing the chapels, which are eight varas and a half in depth.
The middle nave is fourteen varas and a half wide, the other two
each ten and a half. If we allow three varas for the space occupied
by the pillars, we find that the three naves and two rows of pillars
dividing the church have a total width of thirty-eight varas.

" The vaulted roof of each nave is divided into nine bays,
the whole remarkable for solidity and admirable for beauty : two
are behind the principal body. Under the first bay, near the
entrance from the Door of Pardon, stands the monument of the
Holy Week, a wonderful work in three parts : the first rises on
eight columns with its intervals and ovals of extraordinary architecture. The three parts of this sacred mausoleum, constructed
wholly of polished white marble, with gilded profiles, and on which
all the resources of art have been lavished, attain the height of
twenty-two varas. On the platform of the first part, which is reached

by four flights of nine steps each, the services of the holy days are celebrated.

"The middle nave, on reaching the choir, meets the vault which forms the centre of the cross and measures forty-five feet square. It is flanked by the four bays of the transepts, at the end of which are the two magnificent side-doors of the church, which are fifteen feet wide by thirty in height; one is the southern door, which admits the cool air and light, and leads into the cathedral yard, extending for a width of thirty-six feet, all along the church, and continued, but with a width of thirty feet only, towards the apsis on the eastern side, where there are two other doors corresponding with the lateral doors of the principal front : the second door of the transept opens on the *Patio de los Naranjos* (Court of Orange-trees), precisely like that of the same name at Seville.

" The bays of the principal nave which come next comprise the space occupied by the choir, which, like that of Seville, is twenty-four varas in length by thirteen and a half wide. It is furnished with remarkable stalls, all sculptured in precious wood, such as cedar and mahogany, and designed in the purest style of art. There are seventy-five of these seats, high and low, with their entablatures, columns, and mouldings; each back forms a niche, on which are sculptures in full relief representing the Saviour of the World, his Virgin Mother, the twelve Apostles, the Evangelists, the doctors of the Greek Church and of the Latin, the Pontiffs and the Patriarchs of the two communions, — the whole surmounted by capitals, architraves, cornices, etc. The Archbishop's seat is larger in size, more abundantly and more richly sculptured, than those of the canons, and its back is higher. The iron screen at the entrance of the choir opposite the high altar is a remarkable conception; it is of the Corinthian order, and the inner side differs from the outer. Curiosity finds ample gratification in the midst of all these beauties, the wonderful execution of which the beholder feels unable sufficiently to admire.

" On ascending five steps we come to the sanctuary and the high altar, which is raised fifteen feet above the floor of the church : it

is of an imposing size, as becomes the celebration of the holy services and the majesty of divine worship. Against the first two pillars
supporting the vaulted roof are fixed two desks which receive the
missal when the epistles and gospels are chanted. On the altar stands
a very admirable tabernacle, of an octagonal form, surrounded with
ornaments cut in openwork. This tabernacle is formed of two parts
and is surmounted by a superb finial. On the principal festival days
it is covered with a splendid decoration, consisting of pedestals,
columns, cornices, and a cupola, of massive silver, the whole
proportioned to its dimensions. The sanctuary is surrounded with
handsome iron palisading. On each side of the altar, there is a
flight of eleven steps for the use of the priests and other officiating
ministers.

" In the second bay behind the choir, stands the image of *Nuestra Señora de la Antigua,* so famous for miracles, and so attractive for devout persons on account of the beauty of her chapel,
which is a copy of *Los Remedios,* at Seville. Indeed, the plan of
the metropolitan church of Lima was almost entirely copied from
that of Seville. The resemblance between the two churches therefore strikes every body. Each of them has nine doors and numerous chapels under the invocation of the same saints; but if one of
these edifices surpasses in extent, the other has the advantage in
richness of ornament.

" In the immense crypt under the choir is a very spacious vault
divided into three compartments, and which is entered by two doors
in the side naves. In the walls of this vault, recesses have been
made to be used as burial-places for the archbishops : the viceroys
were formerly interred there. In this pantheon is preserved the
head of Francisco Pizarro, also the remains of his daughter Fran-
cisca, who bequeathed considerable property to pay for the daily
celebration of mass at the high altar : the cost of ornaments and the
other expenses occasioned by this mass are paid with the interest
of one thousand gold piastres left for the purpose."

In the church and vestries there are paintings of great merit.
Here are also preserved a piece of the True Cross sent by Pope Ur-

ban VIII., and the relics of St. Julian, St. Sebastian, St. Adrian, St. Marina, St. Saturninus, and St. Faustus, all martyrs.

Among the paintings most deserving of notice, there is a fine portrait of St. Veronica, bequeathed to the church by Archbishop Luna-Pizarro; this portrait, the work of the celebrated Murillo, for which as much as 5,000 piastres had been offered to its owner, hangs in the chapel of Santo Toribio.

The same Señor Luna also presented to the Cathedral another gift equally valuable and useful, being a fine organ, undoubtedly the best in South-America: it was ordered in Belgium, and cost, including its erection in the choir, about 16,000 piastres.

Of all the prelates who, since the Independence, have ascended the archiepiscopal throne, Señor Luna has undoubtedly done most to win the respect of his fellow-citizens.

This church was erected into an episcopal see under the invocation of St. John the Evangelist, by a bull of Pope Paul III., on the 14th of May 1541, published at Lima on the 17th of September 1543 by the first bishop, Dr. J. Geronimo de Loaiza. In 1545, it became the metropolitan church.

The solemn festivals celebrated in the Cathedral, in presence of the members of the Government and the other authorities, are the following : Candlemas, Ash-Wednesday, Palm-Sunday, Maundy-Thursday, Good-Friday, St. Joseph, Easter-Sunday, the anniversary of the Independence, the Assumption (sermon by the Archbishop), St. Rosa (ditto), the Immaculate Conception, the anniversary of the battles of Junin and Ayacucho, and Christmas Day.

The metropolitan chapter consists of the Archbishop and the Dean, the Archdeacon, the Precentor, the Master of the School and the Treasurer, six Canons, four Prebends, and four Semi-Prebends. The synod is composed of ten Examiners presided by the Archbishop.

PARISH-CHURCHES.

The Sagrario and Chapel of Ease of the Orphans. — In describing the Cathedral we mentioned the Court of Orange-trees, where stood, before the last rebuilding of the temple, lodgings for the first sextons, a house for the accountant, and the great Chapter-hall, ornamented with a handsome gallery looking on the Plaza Major. In this hall the provincial councils and synods assembled at Lima held their sessions. After the destruction of these buildings, the ground was assigned for the erection of the chapel of the Sagrario, which is used as a parish church, and was built in the time of the Archbishop Don Melchor de Liñan y Cisneros. The Court of Orange-trees was then reduced to one half its original size and only the premises destined for the offices and archives of the Ecclesiastical Court were preserved.

From the first foundation of the Cathedral till 1541, the parochial services were performed by the Dominicans, in memory of which they retain, to this day, in their church, the original baptismal font.

The parish of the Sagrario is very extensive; therefore, to meet the increasing wants of the service, owing to the great number of parishioners, the chapel of ease of the Orphans was erected and its services performed by the first vicar.

The parish church contains eleven altars, and the chapel of ease, five.

Santa Ana and the Chapel of Ease of the Cercado. — This parish was constituted in 1550 by Archbishop Loaiza, in the church of the hospital of *Santa Ana;* the church was burned down in March 1790, and rebuilt as it now stands.

The chapel of ease was founded by the Jesuits in 1572, and was originally served by them; but after their expulsion, it was declared a dependence of *Santa Ana.*

The parish church has eleven altars; the chapel of ease, ten.

San Sebastian. — This parish was formed in 1561 by the same Archbishop Señor Loaiza; the church has thirteen altars.

San Marcelo. — This church also owed its origin to Señor Loaiza, in 1585; there are thirteen altars.

San Lázaro. — The church of this name was founded in the year 1563 for the use of the hospital to which it was then annexed; but,

owing to the frequent inundations which occasionally rendered communications impossible between the upper and lower parts of the
town, Archbishop Santo Toribio ordered, in 1604, that it should
be a chapel of ease to the Sagrario, and that it should be provided
with every thing necessary for the administration of the sacraments.
By a royal decree of 1746, San Lázaro was made an independent
parish. This church has ten altars.

CHURCHES OF EXISTING CONVENTS.

La Merced. — The church and convent of La Merced were built
in 1534 by Hernando Pizarro, brother to the Conqueror, and cost
700,000 piastres. The church has twenty-three altars. Several festivals are celebrated here, the principal, which falls on the 24th September, being that of the Virgin of Las Mercedes, patroness of the
arms of the Republic.

The convent, at first built under the invocation of the Nativity
of Our Lady, was afterwards called *de la Madre de Dios de la Mer-*

Imp. Godard, rue Jardinet 17, Paris

cea, Redencion de Cautivos (of the Mother of God of Mercy, Redemption of Captives), and the first fathers of the order who came to Peru were Father Osenes and Friar Martin de Victoria. The first mass ever said in Lima was celebrated by Father F. Antonio Bravo of La Merced.

San Agustin. — This church was built in 1554. Archbishop Loaiza laid the first stone, and the whole of the cost was defrayed by Hernan Gonzales de la Torre and his wife Donna Juana Cepeda. The church has sixteen altars. The principal festival celebrated here is that of the patron saint, on the 28th of August.

The first Augustine monk who come to Lima, in 1548, was Father Agustin de la Trinidad; his object was to prepare lodgings for twelve friars of his order, who were to found a community, and they arrived at Callao toward the end of May 1551.

The Augustine friars celebrated their first mass on the festival of St. John the Baptist in a poor little oratory which Father Agustin fitted up in his lodgings, and the first public mass on the 2nd July, the festival of the Visitation of the Virgin Mary.

San. Francisco. — This convent was founded on the same day as the capital, at the instance of the father of the order, Fernando de la Cruz. The church has twenty-six altars. Within the convent there is a house for devotional exercises.

The first site assigned to Father de la Cruz for the Franciscan convent was outside the city and very limited. The friars applied to the viceroy, the Marquis de Cañete, for a more suitable place, and he offered to give them whatever ground they could inclose in one night. Acting on this promise, the monks collected the necessary materials, and in the short time allowed, they raised two fences, one of which completely stopped up a street, and thus inclosed a whole *manzana* (square lot of ground) containing an orchard and a large pond.

The municipality protested against this act as an encroachment on their rights, and demanded that the street should be restored to them, but the viceroy, who wished to favour the Franciscans,

had the ground in question valued and paid for it out of his own purse.

The church and convent of the Franciscans are the most sumptuous in Lima, both internally and externally. The altars are rich and of modern construction.

Los Descalzos. — The church and convent of the *Descalzos* (Barefooted Friars) were founded in 1592 by Father Andrés Corzo, at the foot of Mount San Cristobal. The church has ten altars; in the convent there is a house of devotional exercises for men.

The friars of this convent enjoyed certain revenues, but when the Missionary monks took charge of it in 1852, they gave up the revenues in order to live in the strict observance of their rules. St. Francisco Solano belonged to this convent.

Santo Domingo. — The Dominican friars were the first ecclesiastics who landed in Peru. Pizarro had seven monks of this order in his suite and among them Father Vicente Valverde, who makes a

View of the first Cloister of the Dominican Convent.

very prominent figure in the history of the conquest of South-America.

On the very day of the founding of Lima, Pizarro gave the Dominicans a site for a convent. But, being occupied with the service of the Cathedral and the administration of the sacraments, the friars lived for some time close to that edifice in reed huts of their own building.

The King of Spain, in 1549, confirmed the different donations of land made by Pizarro to the Dominicans, on which have been erected the magnificent convent and majestic temple which now exist.

The church has ten altars. A great number of festivals are celebrated in it, of which the most important are those of Our Lady of the Rosary.

The first prayers said in Lima, the first mass celebrated in the Cathedral, the first sacraments administered, were all by the Dominican friars, and as a souvenir of the first administration of the sacraments they still retain (as already mentioned) the original baptismal font.

Recoleta Dominica (1). — This convent, a dependency of the

.(1) This name was applied to another convent founded by the Dominicans.

preceding, was founded in 1606, by Father F. Juan Lorenzana, provincial of the order of St. Dominic.

The church has thirteen altars.

The foundation was made under the invocation of the Blessed Magdalen, and at its origin the convent did not admit revenues of any sort, for the friars were bound to beg their food from door to door.

Congregation of St. Philip Neri. — This church, known by the name of *San Pedro,* was founded in 1598, for the purpose of celebrating masses for the patients in the hospital of *San Pedro* which then stood on the spot now occupied by the house of the *Recogidas* (recluses).

After the expulsion of the Jesuits, which took place in 1767, the building called the *Colegio Maximo de San Pablo* (High College of

St. Paul), was given to the Congregation of St. Philip Neri, already organized as far back as 1685, and there the fathers of that body still reside.

The church contains seventeen altars. The chief festivals there are those celebrated by the brothers of the confraternity of *Nuestra Señora de la O*, and that of *Gloria*, on Holy Saturday.

The church of *San Pedro* is one of the most sumptuous in the capital; it is of immense size, and contains a great number of artistic beauties.

Buena Muerte (1). — The convent of the *Agonizantes* was erected on premises situated in the Calle de Rufas given for the purpose by Don Antonio Velarde y Bustamante, on the 31st October 1710; and Donna Mariana del Castillo, widow of Don Pedro Bravo de La-

gunas, declared herself protectress of the chapel. At her death, this lady gave her house to the community, and on its site the present convent and church were built.

The church has seven altars. The most remarkable festivals celebrated there are those of St. Camillus, on the 15th of July, and of the Octave of Corpus Christi.

(1) Happy Death.

CHURCHES OF EXISTING MONASTERIES.

Encarnacion. — This was the first convent of nuns established at Lima. Its foundresses were Donna Mencia de Sosa, and her mother Donna Leonor Portocarrero. The retirement of these ladies was made in their own dwelling-house, in which they cloistered themselves rigorously, and assumed the habits of Augustine nuns. Se-

veral other pious ladies having joined them, they finished an edifice appropriate for a monastery, on the 25th May 1558, the festival of the Incarnation, and gave their house the name of *Nostra Señora de los Remedios*.

The church has nine altars.

Concepcion. — This convent was founded in 1573 by Donna Inés Muñoz de Rivera, widow of the commander Don Antonio de Rivera, and by Donna Maria Chavez.

The church has seven altars.

La Trinidad. — Founded in 1580 by Donna Lucrecia Sauzolas and her daughter Donna Mencia de Vargas.

The church has ten altars.

Santa Clara. — Founded by Santo Toribio in 1596. Though the order of these nuns is Franciscan, they follow the rules of the Clarisas of the Observance.

The church has nine altars.

Santa Catalina. — Founded in 1624, by Donna Lucia Guerra de la Daga and her sister Donna Clara, aided by Don Juan Robles, priest and majordomo of the Cathedral.

The church has ten altars.

Descalzas. — This convent of barefooted nuns was founded in 1603 by Donna Leonor Rivera; her sister Donna Beatrix de Orosco, as well as other pious persons, contributed considerable sums for the purpose.

The church has ten altars.

Prado. — Built in 1640 by Donna Angela de Iriarte y Rosalde, a nun of the Incarnation, which monastery she left with four other nuns to found this new one.

Carmen (Carmel). — Founded in pursuance of the royal permission granted· to Don Diego Majuelo, in 1625; towards the expense

this same gentleman, as well as Donna Catalina Daria, Don Miguel Bobadilla, and other persons, contributed important sums.

The church has seven altars.

Trinitarias. — Founded in 1682 by Donna Anna de Robles.

The church has nine altars.

Nazarenas. — The founding of this monastery was approved by a bull of Pope Benedict XIII., promulgated in 1727. It was opened on the 18th March 1730. The first persons who entered it were

three nuns taken from the convent of the *Descalzas* by the viceroy, the Marquis de Castel Fuerte.

The church has seven altars.

Capuchins of Jesus Maria. — This convent was founded at the instance of Maria Jacinta de la Santísima Trinidad. Five Capuchin nuns came from Madrid to settle in it, in conformity with royal letters issued in 1698, 1699, and 1709.

The church has eight altars.

Mercedarias. — This convent was founded, in 1723, with money supplied by Donna Ana de Medina and her daughters, Donna Tomasa de la Cruz and Donna Bernarda de la Madre de Dios, who had previously formed a house of this order.

Santa Rosa. — Founded, in 1708, at the instance of several nuns living in a house called *Rosas de Santa Maria*. Donna Helena

Rodriguez de Corte-Real contributed 130,000 piastres towards the expense.

The church has eight altars.

CHURCHES OF EXISTING BEATERIOS (BEGUIN-HOSUES).

Beaterio de Amparadas. — Founded in 1670 to receive penitent females. The chapel has seven altars.

Beaterio de Viterbo. — Founded in 1680. Its church has seven altars.

Beaterio del Patrocinio. — Founded in 1688. Its church has eight altars.

Beaterio de Copacabana. — Founded in 1691. Its church has nine altars. This house was intended exclusively for the education of Indian girls.

Its origin is said to be as follows: The Virgin of Copacabana was adored in a small hermitage situated in the *Cercado* (outskirts) of Lima. One morning the hermitage was found unroofed, and the

Virgin covered with profuse perspiration. The most illustrious Señor Santo Toribio then had the Virgin carried to the Cathedral, where she remained, all the services of her worship being performed by a brotherhood of Indians, until the year above-mentioned, when the chapel and beaterio were founded at the expense of Don Francisco de Escobar.

PUBLIC CHAPELS OF REGULAR MONKS.

La Vera Cruz. — Annexed to the church of St. Dominic, and founded by Pizarro in 1540. Many curious relics are preserved here.

La Soledad. — Annexed to St. Francisco.

Las Reliquias. — Situated inside the convent of San Agustin.

El Sr. de Consuelo (the Lord of Consolation). — Situated in the portal of the convent of San Agustin.

El Sr. de los Afligidos (the Lord of the Afflicted). — In the cemetery of the church of La Merced, on the side facing the Calle de Jesus Nazareno.

OTHER PUBLIC CHURCHES AND CHAPELS.

Los Desamparados (the Forsaken). — This church, situated in the small square of the same name, formerly belonged to one of the principal Jesuit convents. It was built in 1630 by Father Castillo.

El Espiritu Santo. — A dependency of the old hospital of the same name, intended for sailors; founded in 1571 at the instance of an old mariner named Miguel de Acosta.

La Caridad (Charity). — Annexed to the old hospital of that name, situated in the Plaza de la Constitucion (formerly, *de la Inquisicion*). It was founded by the confraternity of Charity on an estate given for the purpose by Donna Ana Rodriguez de Solorzano. Great ravages made in the capital by an epidemic, in 1559, were the cause of its foundation.

San Carlos. — Annexed to the college so called, was built in 1597. The Jesuits long occupied the college as a house of probation for their novices.

Nuestra Señora del Rosario de abajo del Puente (Our Lady of the Rosary below Bridge). — This is said to be the first chapel erected on the other side of the Rimac.

Naranjos. — Founded by Don Juan Garazatua on the 7th of January 1767.

Sanctuary of Santa Rosa. — In this building, which was formerly a Dominican convent, there are two churches — one outside, belonging to the order; the other inside, built on the spot hallowed by the birth and death of *Santa Rosa de Santa Maria,* the glorious patroness of Lima and of all America.

In this last church, precious relics of that saint are preserved.

Las Cabezas. — Originally founded in 1615, and rebuilt in 1639 by the Father Inquisitor Don Antonio Castro del Castillo.

San Lorenzo. — Begun by order of Don Lorenzo Encalada in 1786, and finished in 1834 by Dr. Don Lorenzo Soria, from his own resources.

Copacabana del Cercada. — Formerly an Indian hermitage, and from it the miraculous sweating statue of the Virgin was removed, in the year 1596, to the Beaterio of the same name.

Cocharcas. — Annexed to a small convent founded in 1681 by a native named Sebastian Alonzo, to receive and educate the sons of the caciques. The first church stood on a spot opposite the site of the present one, which was built in 1777.

Baratillo. — Situated in the small square of the same name, below the bridge; it was erected in 1635.

HOUSES OF DEVOTION FOR MEN.

These, as already stated, are situated inside the convents of the Franciscans and Descalzos and were founded, the first at the request of Father Miguel Echevarria in 1738, and the second by San Francisco Solano.

HOUSES OF DEVOTION FOR WOMEN.

Casa del Corazon de Jesus (Heart of Jesus). — Founded under the direction of the Jesuits in the year 1754.

Casa de Santa Rosa. — Built with property left for the purpose by Donna Rosa Catalina Vazques de Velasco y Peralta.

CHURCH OF THE MONKS HOSPITALLERS.

The only one remaining in Lima is the Iglesia del Refugio, built by the Bethlemite Fathers when they took charge of the hospital to which it is annexed.

CHURCHES OF SUPPRESSED CONVENTS.

Santo Tomás. — Founded in 1645, dependent on the old college of the same name intended for teaching the sciences constituting the educational curriculum of the Dominicans. The convent was once splendid, but is now almost destroyed.

Guadalupe. — Annexed to the convent of the same name, which, since the suppression of the monks, has been used as barracks. It is near the Porta de Guadalupe. In 1611 Don Alonso Roman Cervantes and Elvira de la Serna built a hermitage on this spot, which they subsequently transferred to the Franciscans to become the site of the college of San Buenaventura, and the friars erected the college and church. This last has been recently renovated by Colonel Don Juan N. Vargas.

Belen (Bethlehem). — Founded in 1604 by Donna Paula Pilardo; it contains nine altars.

Santa Liberata. — Founded in 1711 by the viceroy, Ladron de Guevara, because at this spot were found some consecrated wafers, enclosed in the holy pyx, which had been stolen from the Sagrario. It has seven altars.

San Francisco de Paula Viejo (Old St. Francis de Paula). — Situated in the Calle de Malambo and formerly known by the name of *Nuestra Señora del Socorro*. It has seven altars. This church is in a dilapidated state, and service is seldom performed in it.

San Francisco de Paula Nuevo (New St. Francis de Paula). — Founded in 1794 by the monks of that order; it is in the same street as the preceding, and has eleven altars.

San Pedro Nolasco. — Founded in 1626 by Father Juan Vallejo, provincial of La Merced; it stands in the street of the same name, and has seven altars.

Monserrat. — Built by two lay Benedictines on ground given for the purpose by Donna Maria Loaiza and with funds supplied by Don Antonio Perez de la Canal; it has five altars.

[HERMANDADES (BROTHERHOODS).

In the churches and chapels divers brotherhoods or confraternities have been established, of which the principal are :

The Congregation of Nuestra Señora de la O. — Founded in the Oratory of St. Philip Neri. This brotherhood receives every year a greater number of members than any other on account of the numerous prayers said for the repose of the souls of deceased brethren. Besides, it yearly expends 500 piastres in portions of 20 pias-. tres each, to be distributed to twenty-five poor persons; 500 piastres for a commemorative anniversary, and 1,000 piastres in two wedding portions of 500 each.

The admission fee for each brother is 70 piastres. This congregation pays for 15,000 masses yearly.

The Archconfraternity of Nuestra Señora de la Purissima. — Founded by permission of Archbishop Loaiza, and organized in 1558. The founders were tailors, and for a long time none but members of their corporation could hold the office of majordomo of the brotherhood. This restriction disappeared in 1699.

The archconfraternity is managed by a general junta of brethren and (by delegation) by a select junta composed of the majordomos, treasurers, deputies, syndics, and the advocate.

Sociedad Vascongada de Nuestra Señora de Aranzazu. — Founded in 1612.

Archconfraternity of Nuestra Señora del Rosario. — Founded in 1562. To give some idea of the former wealth of this brotherhood, we need only make the following extracts from the inventories deli-

vered to the majordomos on taking charge of the property belonging
to it :

WEIGHT OF THE SILVER SERVICE OF THE ALTAR.

	Marcos (1)	Onzas.
El anda (2)..........................	1002	
Twelve lamps	782	
Front of altar........................	207	2 1/2
Virgin's throne......................	411	1
Columns and fittings of tabernacle....	387	2
Doors of ditto.......................	241	
Doors of Virgin's niche	103	5
Four large taper-stands..............	223	3
Six smaller ditto....................	150	1
Arches of the niche.................	152	4
Twenty mayas (3)....................	202	

The Remonstrance contained :

Diamonds...........................	1304
Rubies..............................	522
Emeralds...........................	1020
Amethysts	45
Topazes............................	2
Pearls..............................	121

The Virgin's crown :

Diamonds.............	102
Rubies..............................	102
Emeralds...........................	150
Diadem in brilliants.................	3
Rings in brilliants...................	20
Ditto with small brilliants...........	4

By a recent decree the Government has ordered that all the property of the brotherhoods shall be managed by the *Beneficencia*
(Poor Relief Board).

In the churches above enumerated four hundred and fifty-nine
festivals are celebrated every year, and 39,607 masses are said, of
which 19,506 are paid for by the brotherhoods.

(1) The *marco*, of eight *onzas*, was equal to ten ounces troy.
(2) A kind of hand-barrow for carrying relics of saints.
(3) Long silver handles by which the taper-stands were carried.

In all the churches mass is said nearly every day, but always on holydays. The hours are from six in the morning to one in the afternoon. In the church of St. Peter, on festivals, mass is said every half hour at the expense of the Congregacion de la O.

The total number of persons employed in religious services or in taking care of the churches, including priests and nuns, is 1,736.

PART III.

GOVERNMENT OFFICES AND PUBLIC ESTABLISHMENTS.

Administration. — The Chief of the Republic has five ministers or secretaries of state : for foreign affairs; for government, police, and public works; for justice, charity, public instruction, and worship; for finance and commerce; for war and marine. The offices of all five are in the palace.

Lima, as capital of a department, is the residence of the prefect, and as capital of a province, of the sub-prefect and intendant of police.

From 1839 to 1857 municipalities were in abeyance. The first municipal council met at Lima twelve days after the founding of the city. The alcaldes were Nicolas de Rivera the Elder, and Juan Tello, companions of Pizarro.

The municipality is charged with the urban police, the embellishment and salubrity of the city; the alcalde has the superintendence of all public spectacles.

Besides these functions, the municipality keeps the *registro del estado civil*, or registry of all births, marriages, and deaths which occur within its district.

The *Post-office* was established at Lima in 1772, and great improvements having been made in its organization and management, its services are now conducted with tolerable regularity.

The *Court of Accounts* was instituted in 1607 under the name of *Contaduria-general de Valores;* its functions are confined to examining and passing the accounts presented every year by all the administrators of the public revenues.

The *Mint* was established in 1565; it is now provided with all the most improved machinery for coining.

The *General Treasury* was created the same day as the capital was founded. This office receives all the state revenues collected in the capital and makes all payments ordered by the Government through the medium of the ministers.

The *General Direction of Finance* keeps the general account of the receipts and expenditure of the whole Republic.

The *General Direction of Public Credit* was founded in 1826 under the name of *Caja* (Bank) *de Consolidacion.* It was reorganized in 1855 and empowered to collect all moneys intended for the redemption of the public debt and the payment of the interest thereon; it keeps the accounts of the export and sale of guano, and intervenes in all operations connected with the public debt, internal or external.

Justice is administered in Peru by ordinary and special tribunals. The former are :

The *Tribunals of the Peace,* instituted by a provisional regulation of the 10th April 1822, replacing the old corregidors by justices of the peace. Their jurisdiction extends only to limited districts and to civil and criminal matters of trifling importance.

The *Tribunals of First Instance,* instituted at the same time to replace the old alcaldes, have jurisdiction over a province and try all sorts of causes in first resort.

The *Superior Courts,* created by the political constitution of 1823.

The Court of Lima, organized in 1821 under the name of *High Chamber of Justice,* replaced the Royal Audience created by royal letters patent in 1543, which ordered that the tribunal existing at Panama under that name should be removed to Lima. The superior courts hear appeals from judgments of the tribunals of first instance in their respective districts.

The *Supreme Court* was founded by an article of the constitution above-mentioned. It hears appeals from judgments of the superior courts.

The special tribunals, entitled *eclesiástico*, *de aguas*, *de minas*, *de comercio* and *de hacienda*, respectively take cognizance, as their names imply, of suits connected with the church, with rivers, mines, trade, and finance.

Houses of Detention. — *Carceletas*. This prison is the building in which the *Holy Inquisition* used to torment, for the greater glory of God, *persons possessed of the devil, and sorcerers*. Its architecture is therefore of a stern character, as befitted its primitive destination.

It is now used as a place of confinement for persons accused of any offence whatever, but the public voice loudly demands that it be replaced by a prison more in harmony with the present state of civilization in Peru.

Police Prison. — Here are the offices of the Intendant of Police. The building contains several wards for the reception of persons arrested for vagrancy, drunkenness, breaches of the peace, the infringement of police regulations, and offences against public decency. The persons apprehended by the police, if to be sent for trial, are removed to the *Carceletas,* and placed at the disposal of the judicial authorities.

Penitentiary. — The first stone of this building, which, undoubtedly, is one of the best of its kind in South-America, was

External view of the Penitentiary.

laid on the 31st of January 1856, by the Grand Marshal Don Ramon Castilla, president of the Republic.

Don A. Mimey, the architect, drew the plan after the model of the best prisons in the United States.

The front and the whole of the first story are built of granite.

The prison contains three hundred and twelve cells for prisoners; two subterranean passages, by which the governor, unseen, can reach the centre of each ward; offices for the administration, with various dependencies; work-rooms for the prisoners, a chapel, a refectory, kitchens, etc.

The average number of prisoners is 220.

Establishments of Public Instruction. — *The Royal and Pontifical University of San Marcos* was founded by royal decree in 1551. This was the first literary body organized in the New-World, and was indebted for its success to the persevering efforts of the Dominican friars, who supported it from the beginning.

The building was erected in 1576. It contains the hall now used for the sittings of the Chamber of Deputies, which was formerly the chapel; the secretary's offices and archives of the Congress; a hall appropriated to the Medical Society; also a general hall for the University proceedings, and which is likewise used as a place of meeting for the College of Advocates. In this hall there are 92 low seats and 73 higher, besides two galleries, one of them for the canons, the other for the ladies. Its architecture, though old, is substantial and handsome. The upper part of the walls is entirely covered with portraits of former professors and rectors, among whom are some persons of distinguished literary merit.

For some years past no lectures have been given in the University and the title of professor is purely honorary.

At present, and in virtue of the last regulation of the Minister of Public Instruction, the University no longer holds the exclusive right of conferring degrees, which may now be obtained in the schools of Medicine and Law.

In the days of its splendour, the University counted among its members men eminent in literature and science, and the examina-

tions for the degree of doctor were exceedingly severe. The rectors were also very scrupulous as to the personal qualities of the candidates; none but those of gentle birth and honourable conduct could aspire to a seat in that *temple*. The last but one of the Protomedicos (1) of Peru, Dr. Don José Manuel Valdès, was pre-eminent in his day as a scientific physician and a mystical poet; but his great merits were not sufficient to induce the University to receive him into its bosom. He was obliged to visit Madrid and solicit from the king the permission which was refused to him in Peru, as a man of colour; and the king, after due inquiry, deigned to grant it. Dr. Valdès was therefore the first coloured man who graduated in Lima. Since then similar honours have been obtained by men of darker hue and less brilliant talents.

Faculty of Medicine of the University of Lima. — The old *protomedicato* (university council), which underwent divers changes after its institution in 1570, was converted, by a supreme decree of the 9th September 1856, into a Faculty, composed of the professors of the School of Medicine, with a dean as president.

The attributes of this Faculty consist in managing the School, in promoting the progress and extension of the medical sciences, in examining the students, who, after following the courses, wish to be received as physicians, surgeons, pharmaceutic chimists, dentists, and phlebotomists, in delivering their respective diplomas, and in testing the acquirements of foreign physicians.

The last protomedico and first dean of the Faculty was the eminent citizen Dr. D. Cayetano Heredia. Never did any man display greater zeal and self-denial in promoting the best interests of his profession. Having been a pupil of the School of Medicine, he devoted his whole life, and whatever fortune he possessed, to raising medical science in Peru to a height that should do honour to his country. Before Dr. Heredia assumed the direction of the Medical College, the students had received but very superficial instruction. He modified the course of study, introduced the different branches of the

(1) The *protomedico* was the president of the council of examiners, and exercised certain judicial functions over the medical body.

natural sciences, such as chemistry, and other accessories indispensable to the healing art. He formed a rich cabinet of natural history and of apparatus and machines for teaching physics; he established a course of medical and surgical clinics — in short, he gave new life to scientific studies and opened for them a career of real and certain progress.

Nor were these, though so great, all the services rendered to his country by Dr. Heredia. Each of the students was to him the object of most affectionate solicitude. The intellectual capacity of a youth was an all-powerful recommendation to the heart of this eminent man, who paid, from his own purse, the college expenses of many a promising student, and supplied others with the means of improving themselves in Europe. Medicine in Peru is greatly indebted to Dr. Heredia, and many physicians now flourishing owe all their success to his generous efforts.

It is but just, however, to state that Dr. Heredia was assisted by the efficient cooperation of some of the professors, his colleagues, and of this number is the eminent Dr. Manuel Solari, one of the most learned and most illustrious foreign physicians who have practised in Peru.

The death of Dr. Heredia was an event which caused deep sorrow throughout the Republic, and the students, as well as the physicians for whom he had been at college a father, a master, and a rector, gave proofs of their affection and gratitude. The doctor's remains were carried on the shoulders of the students (a thing never before witnessed at Lima), from his residence to the church, and thence to the cemetery, followed by an immense concourse of people. Speeches were delivered over his grave, and abundant tears were shed, not like those which every death draws forth, but such as only flow from hearts oppressed by overwhelming grief.

The tribute paid, in these pages, to the memory of Dr. Heredia also comes from the heart of a pupil who loved and admired him.

School of Medicine. Founded, in 1810, by the viceroy Abascal, under the name of *Colegio de San Fernando,* which was afterwards changed to that of *Colegio de la Independencia,* and to its present name when the Faculty of Medicine was organized. It is governed by the dean, and the members of the Faculty are the professors of the different branches included in the course of medical instruction.

Front view of the School of Medicine.

The professorships of the Faculty can only be obtained by competition, and the trials of capacity to be undergone by candidates are : a written composition , an oral composition, and oral argumentation; the judges afterwards decide by ballot which of the competitors best deserves the chair.

Illustrious College of Advocates. — Founded in 1808. Its chief functions consist in examining candidates for the bar. One of the members, who presides over the corporation, is the director of the practical conferences on jurisprudence.

College of San Carlos. This college, lodged in the premises which were formerly the noviciate of the Jesuits, was founded in 1770, and the colleges of St. Martin and St. Philip were incorporated with it.

The Faculties of philosophy and letters, of mathematics and of the natural sciences are established in this college.

Each Faculty is composed of the rector, its titular professors, and the secretary.

4

The course of philosophical and literary studies extends over five years.

Collegian of San Carlos.

College of Our Lady of Guadalupe. Founded, on the 7th February 1841, on the premises of the old Tobacco Monopoly, in the Calle de la Chacarilla, and at first intended only for primary and secondary instruction; but in 1848 certain branches of jurisprudence were added to its curriculum. In 1855, the Government took charge of the college as a national establishment, and assigned it a revenue; it has ever since been devoted to preparatory and secondary instruction.

Ecclesiastical Seminary of Santo Toribio. This college was founded in 1691 by Archbishop Santo Toribio, and occupied from that time premises situated in the street of the same name.

In the course of 1859, it was transferred into a part of the convent of St. Francis, having its principal entrance in the Calle del Milagro. The erection of the new building, convenient, well-planned, and spacious, cost 60,000 piastres, which sum had been saved for

the purpose by the strict and persevering economy of the late Archbishop Luna-Pizarro.

Costume of a Seminarist.

This college is intended for the education of young men who devote themselves to the ecclesiastical career.

Naval Military Institute. The Naval School, or College of Marine,
was established in 1794 by the viceroy Gil de Lemus. The School
suffered much from repeated removals from one building to another, and by changes of organization, until it was re-established
under its present name.

Central Normal School. In order to render elementary instruction
uniform, on the systems recently adopted, the Government decided
to procure from Europe a director and professors for the Central
Normal School to be established at Lima. The old Custom-house
was selected for its seat, and 121,700 piastres were expended in
adapting the buildings for their new destination. The school was
opened on the 1st of June 1859.

School of Arts and Trades. One of the first decrees issued by

View of the gateway at the School of Arts.

General Don José de San Martin, who, though absorbed in the conduct of the war against the Spaniards, did not neglect the political organization of Peru, made arrangements for establishing a school of arts and trades in each departmental capital. This provision,

Exterior view of the court of the School of Arts.

after being repeated in several supreme decrees, was ultimately em-
bodied in a law.

The administration of Marshal Castilla engaged, as director of
this important establishment, Señor Jarrier, who had founded and
long conducted a school of the same kind in the capital of Chili.

The buildings of the old Colegio Real, which had been occupied
as barracks, were selected for the school, and adapted for its use
under the skilful guidance of the director, so that Lima can now
boast of an establishment which does honour to its progress.

The school contains all kinds of machinery, tools, and apparatus
for teaching the different branches of its programme; and, even before opening the courses, certain castings were made there for the
Government, such as had never before been executed at Lima.

The school was solemnly inaugurated last year (1865).

Besides these national institutions, there are also the Colleges of
Santa Teresa and of Midwifery, which will be described among the
charitable foundations.

Public Library. This was the first establishment founded by the
Independent Government in virtue of supreme decrees issued in
August 1821 and February 1822.

The Library at present consists of three rooms, one for reading,
and the two others surrounded with bookcases containing more
than thirty thousand volumes on all sorts of subjects. There is also
a smaller room called the *sala de deposito*.

Among the printed books there are some of great intrinsic importance, and others remarkable for their antiquity and rarity; also
a few manuscripts, some of which are very curious.

Public Museum. The museum of national antiquities and objects
of natural history was founded by supreme decree in 1826, and,
after several removals, is now installed in rooms adjoining the Library. In a country so rich in natural products as Peru, the meagre-
ness of this establishment is really astonishing, and gives but a very
mean idea of the protection afforded to it by the Government.

It contains 5,330 specimens of mineralogy, zoology, antiquities
both Peruvian and foreign, curiosities or objects of art, a very small

number of which are really valuable. The articles connected with science are in the utmost disorder and confusion, no proper classification having yet been made.

Museum and Library of Artillery. Situated in one of the halls looking into the court of the artillery barracks. They were founded in 1854 by General Don Manuel de Mendiburu, and are kept in excellent order.

The Museum contains about two hundred articles, among which are arms of all ages and of various constructions, some of them valuable for their antiquity or exquisite workmanship.

The library consists of about fifteen hundred volumes.

Medical Society. Organized in September 1864, and consisting of physicians associated for the purpose of promoting the progress of science. Its meetings are held in one of the halls of the University. It has an official organ called the *Gaceta Médica,* published at stated intervals.

Cosmografiato. Instituted to promote the study of cosmography as preparatory to that of navigation, but it has hitherto existed in name only. The Chief Cosmographer's labours are confined to the compiling of the calendar and the *Guia politica del Perú.*

Private Colleges and Schools. Of these there are in Lima thirty-two for boys, fifteen for girls, and twenty-three for both sexes. The number of their pupils is 4,716.

Charitable Establishments. — *Sociedad de Beneficencia.* The first *Junta de Beneficencia,* charged with the guardianship and supervision of the establishments founded by public charity for the relief of the sick and indigent, was created and organized in 1825. After undergoing many changes as to its organization and the number of members, it was definitively settled on the present basis in the year 1848.

A permanent junta is formed of the persons yearly elected to fill certain offices, and of the majordomos and inspectors of the various charitable institutions; but the active management is entrusted solely to the last two categories of members.

Hospital de San Andrés. Founded in 1557 by the viceroy Don Andrés Hurtado de Mendoza, in consequence of the representations of Don Francisco de Molina, who, as early as 1552, had begun to relieve a number of sick poor in a house which he hired for the purpose.

This hospital now receives only male patients; it has twelve wards and can accommodate 600 persons. It is kept remarkably clean, and the service is performed by seventeen Sisters of Charity. The average number of inmates is about three hundred.

Santa Ana. Devoted to females, and founded by Archbishop Loaiza in 1549. It is served by thirteen Sisters of Charity. There are twelve wards, capable of containing four hundred patients; but the average number is about two hundred and fifty.

Refugio. — Though the two hospitals for incurables are not under the management of the Junta de Beneficiencia that body appoints an inspector for them because it pays for the small-pox patients who go there to get cured.

The hospital for men was founded in 1669 by Don Diego Cueto, who placed it under the care of the Bethlemite monks on their arrival in the capital. The women's hospital, which is near the other, was founded in 1804 by the viceroy Aviles. The leper-house, which formerly existed near the parish-church of San Lázaro, was incorporated with these two in the year 1822.

The men's hospital has two wards and can receive sixty patients. The women's is of precisely the same extent. The average number of inmates in the two houses is one hundred and ten.

San Bartolomé. This hospital is not supported by the Beneficencia. It was founded in 1646 by Father Vadillo for the reception of sick negroes, but is now exclusively devoted to the assistance of soldiers of the national army. It contains ten wards for privates and one for officers, and can accommodate three hundred patients in all. The service is performed by seven Sisters of Charity. The number of inmates varies according to the strength of the forces stationed at Lima.

College of Midwifery and Lying-in Hospital. Founded by a supreme decree of the 10th October 1826 and organized by another of the 12th May 1830. Every thing connected with obstetrics is taught here, and in the college there is a ward for the reception of women who have not the means of procuring professional assistance in childbirth.

Hospital for deserted Infants. Founded in 1597 by Don Luiz de Ocheda, surnamed *El Pecador*. It has four wards: one for infants at the breast; another serves as an infirmary for children of above seven; the third is the dormitory for girls under two years; and the fourth is an infirmary for children of a similar age.

This establishment is perfectly organized. To the honour of Lima it may be stated that the number of children deserted is exceedingly small as compared with the population, and that very few belong to the white race.

Asylum for Widows of Decayed Tradesmen. This house was founded by Don Juan Ruiz Davila, but the Beneficencia took charge of it in 1848, and has been constantly adding to the number of rooms, which are assigned by lot to the persons presenting the conditions required by the foundation deeds.

In this asylum a school has been opened to teach reading and sewing to the daughters of the women therein residing, and also to those of tradesmen in reduced circumstances.

Asylum of Jesus Nazareno. Founded by Dr. Lorenzo Soria, who, on his decease, transferred the patronage to the Beneficencia.

College of Santa Teresa. Under the title of *Colegio de Santa Cruz de Atocha,* Don Mateo Pastor and his wife founded, in 1569, an establishment for the maintenance and education of deserted orphan girls. It is confided to the care of six Sisters of Charity.

Madhouse. Among the many good works which the Beneficencia has realized within the last few years, none is more important or more praiseworthy than the erection of this asylum for insane persons of either sex.

The building has every requisite accommodation, as baths, laundries, gardens, etc. The management is entrusted to three Sisters of Charity.

General Cemetery. Situated outside the Portada de Maravillas;

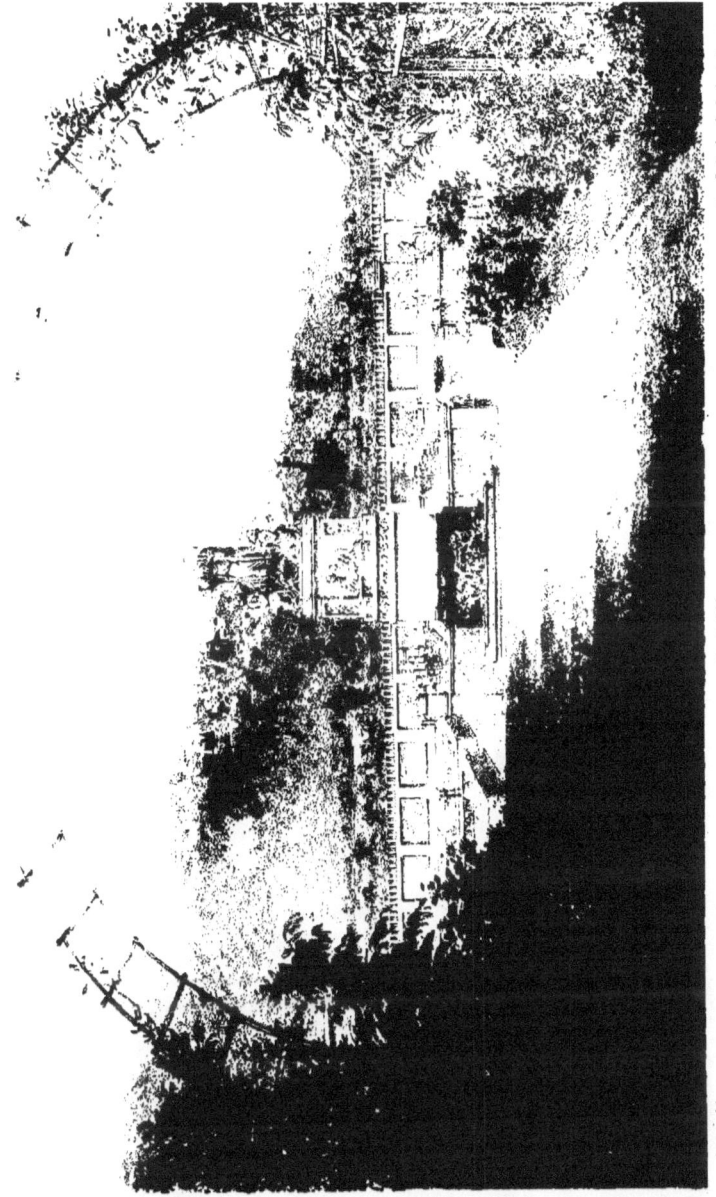

Phot. de P. Memoury

Imp. Godard, r. du Jardinet, /r. ....

Rivière del.

it was planned in 1807, and solemnly inaugurated in June 1808 during the viceroyalty of Señor Abascal. The direction of the works was confided to the priest Don Matias Maestro, a man of exemplary virtue and of very extensive acquirements. The Beneficencia has erected a modest monument to his memory.

Front view of the chapel in the General Cemetery.

The *General Cemetery* is one of the most remarkable establishments of the capital; seen from within or without its aspect is very striking. The Beneficencia has realized great improvements. In all the quarters into which the interior is divided, pretty gardens have been planted and are kept in excellent order. Handsome tombs and sumptuous marble monuments inclose the remains of wealthy persons and of those who have held high office in the Republic, such as Generals Lamar, Gamarra, Salaverry, Necochea, etc.

The altar occupying the centre of the chapel is a magnificent piece of marble executed by a master's hand.

There are in Lima several other benevolent institutions founded by private individuals. The principal are : *The Society of the Founders of the Independence,* the object of which is to assist its members in case of sickness or misfortune, to perform for them when dead all the offices due to the memory of a brother, by assuring to their remains honourable sepulture and by publishing the most distinguished acts of their military life.

This society held its first meeting on the 28th September 1857.
The victors of Junin, of Ayacucho, of the second siege of Callao,
the veterans of the war of Independence, the chaplains and surgeons who served in the armies of their country, are *born* members
of this society; the sons of founders and of veterans are *active*
members, and lastly, the children (of either sex) of *born* members
are *honorary* members.

The *Typographical Mutual Benefit Society* was founded on the
5th of April 1855, for the purpose of aiding those of its members
who may be sick or destitute, and of providing them with a decent
funeral in case of death. All persons employed in printing-offices
may become members on paying the regular monthly subscription.

The *Congregation of the Handmaids of the Poor* was organized
on the 6th July 1856, with a view to relieving the most urgent
wants, as to food, clothes, and medical treatment, of the really
necessitous. Ladies of the highest families in Lima belong to this
association. The *active* sisters are bound to render personal services
and to perform the duties assigned to them.

The *Spanish Charitable Society* was established through the exertions of a Spaniard, Don Francisco J. Moreno, and met for the
first time on the 8th February 1857. Its object is to assist Spaniards
when sick or in distress, to procure work for those who are destitute, or supply them with means to return to Spain. It nevertheless
refuses to aid idle vagrants, persons of bad character, or those who
have been condemned for crimes.

The *French Charitable Society,* which has nearly the same objects
as the preceding, was organized in Lima by several French gentlemen, under the presidentship of M. Edmond de Lesseps, consul-
general and chargé d'affaires of France.

Military Dependencies. — Besides the inspections, garrison staffs,
and military commands, there at Lima two military establishments
deserving of particular notice — St. Catherine's Barracks and Fort,
and the Gunpowder Manufactory.

St. Catherine's Fort, which contains the head-quarters of the artillery, the military museum, the park and workshops, was built in 1806 under the direction of the Spanish sub-inspector of artillery, Don Joaquin de la Pezuela.

The fort comprises the magazines and military offices, the armories, depots of ammunition, lodgings for the officers and sleeping-rooms for the soldiers.

The *Powder Manufactory* was built in the first years of the present century by two private speculators, who began to make powder in 1807, and afterwards supplied nearly all South America and even exported to Spain. In 1826 the Government purchased the establishment and placed it under the dependence of the Corps of Artillery.

The machinery it now employs was obtained from Europe in 1856, at a cost of 90,800 piastres; and for its proper instalment alterations had to be made in the building which entailed an outlay of 130,000 piastres.

PART IV.

General Slaughter-house. — This building, situated a few paces outside the Portada de Monserrat, was erected in 1855 by Don Pedro Conroy, in pursuance of a contract between him and the Government. When the works were finished, Conroy ceded the whole, as well as the rights conferred by his contract, to the State, for the sum of 320,000 piastres. The establishment, having thus become national property, was placed under the immediate management of the municipality, but its proceeds are paid into the General Treasury.

The edifice, though not in the first class of its kind, affords every convenience for the slaughter of sheep and horned cattle.

On an average, the yearly consumption of Lima amounts to 20,390 oxen and 83,330 sheep.

Markets. — The only one worthy of the name is that built, by order of the Government, in 1851, in a part of the convent of the Conception. It cost 244,950 piastres.

This market is attended every day by about one thousand and fifty dealers.

Provisions and comestibles are in general abundant and diversified, with the exception of poultry, of which the supply is very limited in kind. Only fowls and turkeys are always obtainable; there are but few ducks and pigeons, sometimes turtle-doves, very rarely partridges.

Although many kinds of fish are daily brought from Callao and Chorrillos, not more than three or four species are good for much. The *corbina pequeña* (a kind of umber) is the best of them; for some reason unknown, the delicious *peje-rey* (king-fish) has totally disappeared from the coast for several years past.

Pulse and vegetables are abundant and of good quality. The market is supplied from the gardens of the town, or by the Indians of the neighbouring valleys, and the villagers on the coast and in the mountains.

The kinds of meat found in greatest abundance are beef, mutton, and pork. Kids may be obtained in the environs, but not many are brought to market. Rabbits are seldom seen, still less frequently venison, though game is tolerably abundant in the neighbouring valleys.

Railways. — Lima has two railways, one running to Callao, the other to the village of Chorrillos.

The first was made in virtue of a contract concluded by the Government with Don Pedro Candamo, who obtained a privilege for ninety years, at the expiration of which the railway and all the rolling-stock will belong to the Government. On this line the service is very irregular; the managers, in announcing the time of departure and arrival of trains, always add the words *or thereabouts,* in virtue of which they sometimes keep travellers waiting whole hours.

The railway from Lima to Chorrillos was constructed by a company under a concession from the Government. It afterwards passed into the hands of Señor Candamo above-mentioned, who has since sold his interest in both lines to an English company.

Electric Telegraph. — A line was established between Lima and Callao by a private speculator under a concession granted by the Government. It began to work on the 23rd of April 1857.

Hackney Carriages. — There is a stand of coaches plying for

hire in the *Plaza Mayor* at all hours of the day. The number licen-
sed is ninety-six. This useful improvement was introduced in 1858.

Natural Productions of Lima. — It would be a long task to enumerate all the plants raised within the walls of Lima. The ferti-
lity of the gardens and of the soil generally is such that almost anything may be successfully cultivated which does not require either
a very cold temperature or a low atmospheric pressure. There are
indeed but very few plants imported from Europe which an intelligent gardener cannot easily rear on this productive soil.

Among the rarer kinds of flowers, we see in the gardens of Lima
an immense variety of camellias, magnolias, ranunculuses, anemo-
nes, pinks, and carnations, rich in colour and fragrance; roses of
all sorts, lilies, nards, narcissuses, jasmines, especially the Cape jasmine (a tropical flower of most agreeable odour, somewhat resem-
bleng the camellia by its pure white and the size of its petals), violets,
diamelus rallenas, tulips, and many other flowers both indigenous
and exotic.

Among the principal vegetables grown in Lima are : cabbages,
lettuces of many kinds, carrots, turnips, onions, tomatos, parsley,
chicory, artichokes, cauliflowers, etc.

The fruits comprise all those of the torrid and temperate zones,
the principal being : the famous chirimolla (1), various kinds of
plutano, the *granadilla,* the apple, grapes of divers qualities, the
fragrant *palillo,* the *palta,* the *lacuma,* the peach, the sweet orange,
the sweet and bitter lemon, the cherry, the fig, the plum, the straw-
berry, the pine-apple (considered by many the king of fruits), the
medlar, quince, melon, water-melon, and many others not less
esteemed.

As for tame animals, there are the horse, the ass, the dog, the
cat, the rabbit, the guinea-pig, the sheep, the hog, and the goat.

Of the feathered race, there are : the turkey, the peacock, the
hen, the duck, the goose, the pigeon, the canary, the linnet, and
the cuckoo.

(1) A splendid fruit having the external appearance of a green velvet purse, and
containing a white milk of exquisite flavour.

Many other animals, both wild and tame, are brought from the coast, the mountains, or abroad, but do not breed there.

At Lima there are few venomous insects or reptiles; it is a very rare occurrence to find in well-kept houses either scorpions, centipedes, or snakes.

Of the vermin class, rats and mice are exceedingly numerous.

As to noisome insects there are, in certain seasons, plenty of mosquitoes, flies, fleas, bugs, and, in places where proper attention is not paid to cleanliness, chigoes or jiggers.

Commerce and Manufactures. — The capital receives merchandise from nearly all the commercial nations of the world, the importers generally being Europeans. The exports of Peruvian produce are very trifling, but the yearly increase of the imports is considerable.

The capital likewise trades with all the towns of the Republic by sea and land, principally in common woollen tissues, fruits, and other eatables.

Of the European States with which Lima entertains commercial relations, those importing on the largest scale are England and France. The former does the most extensive business in woollen, cotton, and linen goods; the latter in silks, millinery, perfumery, and jewellery.

A careful examination of official documents relative to 1860 shows the value of imports during that year to have been : from Chili, 1,547,402 piastres; from Ecuador, 42,192; from France, 3,199,899; from England, 2,852,218; from North America, 280,489; from Panama, 891,000; from Germany, 751,867; and 450,000 from other countries.

As to the various kinds of merchandise thus imported, cotton goods amounted to 1,347,900 piastres; woollen, to 1,200,000; linen to 192,864; silk to 984,786; ready-made clothes to 794,678; drugs and chemicals, to 84,751; ironmongery and hardware to 392,654; furniture to 242,710; wines and liqueurs to 71,816; provisions to 1,349,799; sundries to 2,755,109.

From the 10,015,057 piastres, the total value of these imports,

Bouvier del

Phot de Couvret frères

Imr Gadard, r En Jardinet 'S P...

must be deducted 829,467 piastres, the value of articles re-exported; so that the actual consumption reaches the sum of 9,187,590 piastres. It was 6,041,293 piastres in 1852, and 7,887,650 in

View of the Port of Callao, from behind the fortress.

1857; from these figures the average annual increase is found to be 349,485 piastres.

The principal port of Peru, the nearest to Lima, is Callao, where, of course, the greater part of the foreign trade is transacted.

Front view of the Callao Customhouse.

The fine bay, being completely sheltered from the winds which assail all the other ports on the Pacific, affords the most perfect security to all kinds of shipping. It is true that the landing-quay for

5

merchandise is not so convenient as might be wished, but we learn that the Government has lately signed a contract for making a new one which will be accessible for ships of the largest size.

The building now used as a customhouse at Callao is the old castle of the Independence, which has been almost entirely dismantled and has undergone many other changes to adapt it for the present purpose.

As the products of Peru, which were formerly bars of silver, in addition to large quantities of hides, wool, saltpetre, cinchona, and minerals, no longer suffice to balance her imports, the greater part of the return cargoes consist of guano, of which there are immense deposits all along the coast of Peru and especially on the Chincha Islands. The enormous sums which these islands, the only parts hitherto worked, have produced since 1844, constitute nearly the whole revenue on which Peru relies to meet her expenditure.

View of the Chincha Islands.

The high price of labour at Lima has prevented that capital from making any progress in manufactures. Several attempts made by adventurous speculators have proved, by their unfortunate results, that it is impossible for goods manufactured in the country to bear competition with those of the same kind imported from abroad. A glass-house and two manufactories for silk and linen tissues were started and kept at work long enough to prove that they could not possibly yield a profit. Providence has, nevertheless, endowed the Peruvians with considerable artistic talents, a fact demonstrated by the sculptures, paintings, and tissues executed even in the mountain districts, where genius is often discovered in spite of the want of scholastic or other instruction.

The tailors, shoemakers, carpenters, and other artisans of Lima work with as much skill and taste as those of Europe, though they cannot practise their craft on a large scale, because of the impossibility of bringing down their prices so low as those of similar articles manufactured abroad.

Among the new arts which have attained the greatest perfection at Lima, photography holds a prominent place. There can be no doubt that the artists there produce proofs every way as perfect as those of the most advanced countries. This may be in some degree due to the powerful auxiliaries of the pure sky and bright sun peculiar to tropical climates. The engravings and lithographs in the present work were copied from photographs taken by MM. Maunoury and Courret brothers, of Lima.

Printing is one of the industrial arts which have made most progress in the last twenty years. For a long time, the printing-office of Don José Marias, established in 1817, was the best in Peru; but in 1839 a formidable rival arose in the office of the *Comercio,* which was organized in a superior manner. In 1852 the office of the *Heraldo* was founded, and executed its work in the best modern style. In 1860 another was set up for printing the *Mercurio,* and this last has certainly become the foremost in all South-America for its organization, as also for the excellence and extent of its founts and the perfection of its machinery.

The building occupied by this office is large and divided into three portions : the first contains the editor's rooms, those of the director, etc.; the second is a spacious hall, surrounded by an upper gallery, the whole forming an admirable composing-room, with frames and cases for sixty compositors. The third part is occupied by the presses for the journals and other work, by the steam-engine which drives them, the wetting-rooms, etc.

Composing-room.

This office became the property of the Government in 1865. After this establishment comes that of Huerta and Co., remarkable for superior workmanship, and in the third place, the *Imprenta Liberal.*

Part of the upper gallery.

Lavieille del.   Fec. de Richardson   Imp. Godart r. du Jardinet 19 Paris

PART V.

PLACES OF PUBLIC AMUSEMENT, WORKS OF ART, AND WALKS.

The Lima Theatre was founded in 1601, and was the property of St. Andrew's Hospital. Since that time, several edifices have been successively erected for dramatic performances, as the first fell to ruin. The present building dates from 1660. It will hold fifteen hundred persons.

Front view of the Lima Theatre.

The Beneficencia used to manage the theatre as being the property of one of the hospitals confided to its care. In 1852, however, the Government undertook the charge on its own account, giving the hospital other property in exchange. Since then, the theatre has

been transferred to the municipality. As a building, it is altogether
unworthy of a civilized nation.

Plaza de Acho. — This vast circus, intended for bull-fights, was
constructed in 1768 by Don Agustin Hipolito Landazuri. It is the

View of the Plaza de Acho on a fight-day.

finest in the world, being of much greater area than the circus of
Pampeluna, which is the largest in Spain. It will accommodate nine
thousand spectators.

In pursuance of the stipulations of the contract under which
Landazuri built this circus, it has now become the property of an
hospital under the management of the Beneficencia.

El Paseo de los Descalzos is a public walk, situated on the other
side of the bridge. It was originally an avenue of trees planted in
1611, but these were cut down in 1856 in order to make a promenade on a new and more beautiful plan.

Its area is 60,623 square varas. In the middle there is a long
avenue nineteen varas in width enclosed by iron palisading brought
from Europe. At one extremity of this garden, there is a basin with
a very lofty jet of water.

Across the end of this enclosure and throughout its whole length
are beds about three varas in width covered with flowering plants and
shrubs which greatly enhance the attractions of the place. By the
side of these plantations are a hundred iron urns on pedestals

De Navarret del.   Imp. Godard . Paris

of the same metal, about two varas in height. There are also
twelve gas-lamps. The internal ornamentation of the avenue is completed by twelve colossal marble statues representing the signs of the
zodiac resting on plinths of a beautiful stone sculptured on the spot.
Outside the palisades is a wide road for carriages and horses,
planted with rows of willows. On the right, stands a graceful pavi-

Front view of Promenade of the Descalzos.

lion surrounded with verdure, where, on certain festivals, a band
of music plays in public. This promenade has cost 119,047 piastres
7 reales.

La Alameda Nueva ó del Acho, made in 1773, is a another promenade, with three alleys : the middle one intended for persons in
carriages or on horseback, the two lateral ones for people on foot; it
is 316 varas in length from the entrance to the Plazoleta del Acho,
in the middle of which stands a beautiful statue of Christopher Co-
lumbus.

This statue, or group, to speak more correctly, represents the
navigator raising the veil which covered the face of a beautiful In-

dian female symbolizing America. It is marble and exquisitely sculptured. The artist was Salvatore Revelli, who received 4,300 piastres
for it. The pedestal and bas-reliefs are by Giuseppe Palombini, and
cost 3,000 piastres.

Exclusive of the freight from Europe to Callao, the outlay for
the group, as it now stands, amounted to 9,953 piastres 5 reales.

Alameda del Callao. — This walk, made in 1797, is now in a
very bad state; its trees have been neglected, its paths broken up,
through being frequently flooded by the overflowing of the water-
courses. There are two rows of willow trees, the right hand one
containing 1451, and the left 1,108.

Equestrian Statue of Bolivar. — In 1858, the 8th of December,
the anniversary of the famous battle of Ayacucho, which for ever
secured the independence of Peru, witnessed the unveiling, in the
presence of the whole people, of the splendid bronze statue erected
by a grateful nation to General Simon Bolivar, one of the men who
did most to secure American independence.

The statue stands in the Plaza de la Constitucion, and the metal
composing it is the same as that of the celebrated statue of Ba-
varia at Munich. The weight of Bolivar's statue is 238 quintales
(nearly 11 tons), and its height, from the horse's hoofs to the rider's
head, 5 varas (13 feet 9 inches English).

The horse is rearing, and consequently supported only by his
hind legs and tail. Bolivar is represented hat in hand, in the act of
saluting. He wears a cloak, but so artistically disposed as to leave
visible his military uniform.

The statue stands on a beautiful marble pedestal with three broad
steps. On the sides are bas-reliefs representing, to the right, the
battle of Ayacucho, to the left, that of Junin. There are two other
bronze reliefs, the one in front bearing the following inscription in
large letters:

A SIMON BOLIVAR
LIBERTADOR
LA NACION PERUANA
AÑO MDCCCLVIII

Ch. Rivierres lith

The other, on the opposite side, presents the national arms. The statue and its erection cost more than 22,000 piastres.

El Paseo de Aguas (the Water Promenade). This public walk was projected by the Viceroy Amat, but left unfinished, and its decorations in masonry are now little better than ruins.

View of the Paseo de Aguas.

PART VI.

How many colours!

We have somewhere read, but cannot say whether in print or manuscript, that "a field totally covered with white flowers would

Indian before the Conquest.

present the same aspect from all points of view; that sameness is monotony; that monotony wearies the senses; that what wearies

the senses is disagreeable, and that consequently a field totally covered with..." The reader may, if he pleases, complete the inference.

If the hypothesis of the field can be applied to populations, that
of Lima must necessarily by pleasing, for it is not composed of
whites only, and therefore is not uniform, or monotonous, or
wearying to the senses.

Every body knows that the inhabitants of Peru, before it had the
honour to be conquered, consisted of one race, the Indian, or as the

Indian since the Conquest (1).

learned say, the yellow race. The conquerors were whites, and the
yellow-white, that is, the mixed offspring of the conqueror and the
conquered, received the designation of *mestizos.*

Those who introduced catholicism into Peru also introduced a friar

(1) Our engraving is an exact copy of a photograph taken from life at Lima. The
original is still living. From his countenance, a perfect type of the Indian, and his
bearing, it is easy to form an idea of the kind of civilization which three centuries of
Spanish rule have imposed on the aboriginals of Peru.

INDIAN WOMAN OF THE MOUNTAINS

Valverde and an inquisition; those who brought us civilization at a later date established slavery, and to speak only of Lima, they imported an immense number of negroes from Africa on whom they also pretended to confer the benefits of civilization and religion, by deceiving and hunting them like wild beasts to deprive them of liberty for life.

From these three colours, types of three different races, proceeded the following combinations: from the white and the yellow (as already stated) the *mestizo;* from the mestizo and the yellow, the *white;* from the black and the yellow (not the green of the painter's pallet, but) what at Lima is called *chino-cholo;* from this last and

China-Chola.

the negro, the *chino-prieto;* from this and the white, the *chino-claro;* from the white and the negro, the *zambo;* from this and the white, the *mulatto;* whose union with the white produces the *cuarteron;* from this last and the white, comes the *quinteron,* whose offspring when married to a white person, is *white.*

The population of Lima therefore presents, in its component

parts, a regular gradation of tints from the deepest and glossiest black to the purest white, and from this last to yellow, so that there can scarcely be any thing like monotony. Since the importation of African negroes ceased, that is, since 1793, the number of pure

Negro of the pure stock.

blacks has greatly fallen off, and the African race has become so scarce as to be represented only here and there by some very old negro.

The negroes at Lima were employed in all kinds of laborious and menial occupations: they were field-labourers, water-carriers, drivers of *calesas* (1), hawkers of fruit, sweetmeats, *tamales* (maize-flour pastry), *humitas* (spiced cakes of maize-flour), etc. The African negro, called *bozal*, on account of his awkwardness, was the most submissive, faithful, and humble servant that can be imagined; though

(1) The old *calesa* (calash) of Lima was very different from the carriages now used there, being much like an old-fashioned English post-chaise, without a box for the driver, as will be seen by the accompanying engraving.

NEGRO WATER-CARRIER

treated rather as a wild beast that a rational being, he would endure the most cruel chastisement with the resignation of a martyr. When the negroes arrived at Lima, the first thought of their new masters was to get them baptized and made catholics. All of them soon became fervent adorers of the *Virgin del Carmen* or *del Rosario,* and assembled, according to their castes, in brotherhoods to deliberate on matters connected with their public worship or on other important business. As these meetings of the negroes exhibit

The old Lima *calesa.*

many peculiar features, we will here introduce a description of them, which we have published in another work (1).

" The principal castes of negroes who serve us are ten in number: the *Terranovos,* *Lucumés,* *Mandingas,* *Cumbundas,* *Carabalies,* *Cangaes, Chalas, Huarochiries, Congos,* and *Misangas.* These names are not all derived from the country from which each caste originally came : some are purely arbitrary, as *Huarochiries,* others are taken from the name of the place where they first staid after landing, as *Terranovos* for instance. All these castes are subject to *coporales-mayores* (corporal-majors) whom they themselves elect, and who hold office for life. The elections take place in the chapel of Our Lady of the Rosary, founded and maintained by the blacks in

(1) *Statistics of Lima,* 1858.

the great Dominican convent. The negroes who take part in the vote are the foremen and *Veinticuatros* (twenty-four) (1) of each caste (we would call them *Senators,* did we not fear to degrade the name). These voters proceed to the election, in the presence of the Father-°Chaplain of the confraternity, and their choice always falls on the oldest amongst them who are descendants of the founders. The name of the individual elected is then entered in a book kept for the purpose, and all this is effected without any intervention of the public authorities.

" The same formalities are observed when a subaltern corporal, or one of the *veinticuatros* is named for each caste in particular; but these on their admission pay as a contribution, the corporal ten pias-tres, and the brother twelve. One moiety of this money goes to-wards the maintenance of the chapel, the other pays for the refresh-ments which are given to the electors, whose decisions are in-scribed in the register above-mentioned.

"These dignities give their possessor great consideration among the persons of his tribe; but as regards his slavery and his labour, they are absolutely null, and procure him no relief whatever. It is really a subject for laughter, or rather for compassion, to see the whilom sovereign of an African nation sent with his subjects to mow-grass at two o'clock in the morning, and sometimes receive from their hands a number of lashes by order of the manager. One of our friends, when at the farm of.***, a few days since, saw a negro with his head in the *cepo* (2), and, having asked his name, could not refrain from tears, on hearing the answer: « *He is the king of the Congos;* » for the kingly name, which we have learned to venerate from our infancy, commands almost sacred respect and awe, even when applied in irony or jest.

" All the castes above-mentioned defray the expenses of the worship of our Lady of the Rosary by an annual contribution of half a real per head, which is paid on the Sunday after Corpus Christi at a table placed for the purpose in the Plazuela de Santo

(1) *Twenty-four*, a name given to the brethren of some confraternities.
(2) *Cepo*, a kind of stocks for confining either the head or feet of offenders.

Domingo, and there is no tradition of a larger sum having been ever offered. But of the total receipts, a sufficient portion is taken to celebrate the annual festival of the holy image, and the rest is devoted to the general purposes of the chapel.

"The expense of funerals is met in the same manner : each family subscribes six reales, and the sum thus collected pays for the masses and the responses for the dead. The corporal-majors receive the remainder, if there be any, and divide it among the subaltern corporals and brethren, who are subordinate in all things to the decisions of the said majors.

" Formerly, the *Terranovos* and *Lacumés* devoted themselves to the image of the Holy Saviour, in the convent of our Lady of Mercy. This devotion is now followed by the *Congo* negroes, whose brotherhood is established in the plantain-grove of St. Francis de Paula, with no other resources than alms voluntarily collected among themselves.

" The *Mandingas* also had a chapel in the church of the great Franciscan convent, dedicated to the Virgin, under the name of our Lady of the Kings. It is now ruined, as are also the other brotherhoods established in the churches of *San Sebastian, Monserrat*, the chapel *del Baratillo*, and another small chapel near the bridge. The negro and mulatto teamsters have a brotherhood at the church of *San Agustin* for the worship of St. Nicholas. The majority of them are creoles (born in Peru); they elect their majordomo with the intervention of the authorities, though they have no funds for the maintenance of the brotherhood but their own voluntary contributions.

" The festival which they solemnize with most pomp is the Sunday after Corpus Christi. All the tribes assemble on that day for the procession, which starts from the great Dominican convent. Each carries its banner and parasol, under which walks the king or the queen, with a sceptre in the right hand and a staff or some other instrument in the left.

" All the rest of the nation follow, playing on noisy instruments, the majority of which make a terrible uproar. The attendant sub-

6

jects, who precede the kings, are dressed in every variety of fright-
ful costume. Some appear us demons, or stuck all over with feathers;
others are wrapped in skins to imitate bears; and others again are
got up as monsters with horns, hawk's feathers, and serpent's tails.
All are armed with bows and arrows, clubs, and bucklers; they paint
their faces red or blue, according to the usage of their countries,
and follow the procession uttering savage yells, and making mena-
cing gestures, as if about to attack an enemy. The seriousness and
ferocious enthusiasm which they display in these scenes, may give
some idea of the barbarity with which they carried on their wars.
This outrageous mummery, which might very well suit a carnival
masquerade, appears altogether unbecoming in a religious ceremonial, and still more in a procession, where the least impropriety
profanes the dignity of the sacred act, and banishes every feeling of
devotion in the spectators. Perhaps our children will witness the
reform of these abuses and others of a like nature, which we heartily desire to see at once suppressed. The authorities have already
wisely forbidden the negroes to discharge fire-arms during the processions, as was the custom formerly.

" All the juntas or assemblies here enumerated begin under the cover of religion to end in others having amusement for their only object. In several streets of the capital the negroes of whom we speak have houses or lodges (sixteen in number, and called *cofradias*) which are their rallying points on festival days. Each tribe has the sole use of one of these places for its meetings, and some of the more numerous have two or three. With money collected from among themselves, they buy ground to build these lodges, and have only to pay a very trifling tax for them.

" The corporal of each caste or nation is the president of the junta, and enforces the strictest etiquette as to seats, which are all classed according to seniority. The *Bozales* negroes, though patient under the rudest field labour, almost indifferent as to the quality of their food, little affected by severe chastisement, and wonderfully intrepid when in danger of the knife or the gallows, cannot endure any injustice or neglect in matters of precedence. To be seated an inch higher or lower will give them the utmost pleasure or deepest chagrin. From the existence of these contrasts, it would seem as if prejudice disputes the preponderance with nature and very often proves the stronger. Here are men who will patiently endure hunger and privations, sleep soundly on hard planks, renounce without a pang all the joys and consolations to be found in civilized society, and yet who tremble with rage, bewail their lot, and think themselves the most miserable of mortals, if on some trifling occasion they happen to get placed on the left instead of on the right; if any one mentions their name without a complimentary epithet, or if in writing it, the letters of which it is composed are not arranged in the wonted order. This kind of mania is found in the very lowest ranks of those whom fortune has devoted to humiliation, hopeless endurance, and all the sternest realities of life. Men who labour under this weakness should feel ashamed thus to find themselves on a level with the Bozales negroes and exposed to the same ridicule.

" The meetings in question begin about two in the afternoon. The first hour is employed in deliberating on matters connected

with the interests of their nation, taking account of the contributions, in settling disputes between husbands and wives, etc. The
corporals explain what use they have made of the money entrusted
to them, and make proposals as to the employment of the balance
in hand. One of the most interesting features which these sittings
present for the philosophic observer is the perfect gravity with
which the chiefs and their subordinates express their opinions,
listen, and obey. Man has no true sense of his dignity until social
bonds and intercourse enable him to compare himself with his
fellow-men. Then he begins to form his character, to respect himself, and to have a higher conception of his being than he had enter-
tained while he lived in the midst of wild animals in the solitudes
of mountains and forests.

" How wonderful also is the rapidity with which negroes pass
from one extreme of stern sedateness to another of brawling, disorder, and extravagance! When their business has been transacted,
they begin to dance, and keep on till seven or eight in the evening.
On all the walls of these lodges, especially inside, are rude paintings representing their imaginary kings, their battles, and carou-
sals. The view of these extravagant pictures excites and delights
them. The observation has often been made that the feasts they
celebrate away from their lodges and far from their paintings are
cold, dull, and soon over. Their balls indeed are not very attractive,
even when they do not offend our notions of decency. When a
negro dances alone, which is most usual, he jumps about wildly in
all directions, turns violently this way and that, never looking
where he is going. All the dancer's skill consists in displaying great
vigour of limb and in making the inflections of his body correspond
with the cadence of the tune sung by the persons forming the circle.
If two or four dance at the same time, the men first place themselves opposite their partners, making a few ridiculous contorsions
and singing; then they turn sideways, gradually separating; at last
they swing round to the right, all together, and then hastily ap-
proach each other face to face. The shock which results from their
collision appears anything but pleasant to persons who believe that

the *Bozales* suffer as much from such violence as white people would. This simple and rude exercise constitutes all their recreation; their dance has no rules or figures except those inspired by the caprice of the moment. But they doubtless amuse themselves, and when the holiday is over, their impressions disappear with it. It would be a great blessing if the more complicated French, English, and German dances were never attended with any worse consequences than weariness and loss of time! Unfortunately they are, but too often, the pretext for amorous intrigues and cause no little scandal.

"We have already remarked that the music of the *Bozales* is extremely disagreeable. The drum is their principal instrument; the commonest sorts are made of a jar or a hollow wooden cylinder, and are not beaten with sticks but struck with the hands.

" They have also small flutes into which they blow with the nostrils. They likewise produce a kind of musical sound by striking the dried jawbone of a horse or of an ass, having moveable teeth; they obtain a similar result by rubbing one piece of smooth wood

against another with notches on the surface. One of their instruments called the *marimba*, has some pretensions to melody. It consists of several thin, long, and narrow slips of wood, fastened, by means of a wooden hoop, across the open end of a dry and empty calabash. It is played upon with short sticks like the old

Bohemian psaltery. As the diameter of the calabash gradually de-
creases from the large end, this instrument has a variety of notes
which are sometimes not altogether unpleasing even to delicate
ears. After all, we are obliged to confess that, with regard to music,
dancing, and many other matters depending on talent and taste,
the negroes are as far inferior to the Indians as the latter are to the
Spaniards.

" When a corporal, one of the twenty-four, or a wife of either
happens to die, the tribe assembles at its usual place of meeting,
and holds a wake over the corpse. The character of this service is
an indisputable proof that the *Bozal* has not changed his nature in
coming to another country, for he retains in our midst, as long as
he lives, his original superstition and idolatry. It is easy to suppose
that he cannot love a country in which he leads such a wretched
existence. How should he not abhor everything which contributes to
enslave him? How should the poor creature raise his mind to the
contemplation of our sublime mysteries, while his eyes and heart
are ever turned earthwards and he seldom succeeds in learning to
understand our language? The chamber of the dead is lighted by
four tallow candles; the children of the deceased sit at the foot of the
coffin; the relatives stand on each side, and occasionally speak to
the corpse. The friends of the family dance and jump around, stopping occasionally to murmur a short prayer in their native tongue,
according to the usages of their forefathers. Each attendant gives
half a real towards the expense of the funeral and to buy drink,
most frequently *guarapo* (1), but sometimes brandy. Before the
drinking begins, a full cup is held near the mouth of the deceased,
and a few words are spoken, as if entreating him to drink. When
he is supposed to have acceded to this request, the cup is passed to
the nearest relatives, scrupulously observing the different degrees
of precedence in every case. After drinking freely, singing and
dancing terminate the ceremonial which began with tears and
lamentations.

_____

(1) *Guarapo*, a fermented beverage made from the residue of the sugar-cane.

" When the widow of a man who has attained the distinction of being a corporal of his tribe wishes to take a second husband, she must declare before the assembly how dearly she loved her first husband and how she has duly mourned his loss. On the day which they call *guitaluto* (last of mourning), they carry her on a seat formed of their joined hands from her home to the lodge of the brotherhood; she enters in tears, and if she does not act satisfactorily the part of a mourner, she is exposed to be flogged with a whip for her hard-heartedness. The moment she crosses the threshold, a lamb is killed on one of the earthen seats of the room as a sacrifice to the manes of the deceased, to whose memory the new bride is about to bid adieu. The woman then presents, on a silver salver, the shoes which she has worn out during her widowhood. After these ceremonies, the civil marriage is celebrated, and all the brethren pay their respects to the happy couple by offering them liquors and viands of all sorts.

" When a widower remarries, none of these conditions are observed. The *Bozales* say *that it is foolish for a man to distress himself about the death of a wife, as there are always a hundred ready to take her place.* If there be anything which proves the degraded state of these unhappy Africans, it is the adoption of this abominable maxim. Just and sensible men think very differently. Among us there are some who believe that the long life of an antediluvian patriarch would be insufficient to lament the loss of a good wife."

The *Bozal* negro soon learned to do any kind of work, and might be employed for any purpose except *doing errands.* The negro would be sure to deliver a message differing from that with which he was charged, if not absolutely contrary to it. The Bozales could never learn to speak the Spanish language with even tolerable accuracy.

The decrease in the number of blacks and the total abolition of slavery in 1855 induced certain speculators to give greater extension to the importation of Chinese coolies intended for domestic service and agricultural labour. Some time previously a number of European labourers had been introduced, but the result was by no means satisfactory. The Chinese however answered the purpose of the importers, who demanded 350 piastres for each subject of the Celestial Empire, but the latter did not altogether replace the African negroes. They are certainly more intelligent and fit for any kind of work, but they are not so healthy nor so fit for hard toil, nor so patient and obedient. On the contrary, chastisement so irritates them, that if they cannot take vengeance on their employer, they will hang themselves with as little hesitation as Englishmen are said to do.

The Chinese are much inclined to culinary manipulations, and many of them have become excellent cooks at Lima, but they have the reputation of not being over cleanly in their operations. On this head, we will relate an incident which happened to one of our friends. He had a Chinese cook, who prepared the *puchero Limeño* (Limanian beef-soup), in perfection. One day, having invited a party of intimate friends to a *creole* dinner, our friend went into the kitchen to see how the *puchero* was getting on, when, having raised the lid of the kettle, he was horrified by seeing a large rat lying on the cabbage. In answer to a severe scolding, the Chinese coolly said : " Do not be alarmed; *puchero* for you, rat for myself. "

The Chinese seldom fulfil the terms of their engagement. With or without reason, they leave the farms or houses where they are employed, and get fresh places, of course at higher wages. At first, the police were called in to fetch back the runaways, but the Chinese themselves have recently established an agency, which undertakes to bring the absconders back to their masters. This however seems to have only had the effect of aggravating the evil; for the agency encourages servants to run away by giving them a moiety of the 25 piastres which the former receives for taking them back.

When the Chinese have fully recovered their liberty, either by indemnifying the importers with a money payment or by duly working out the time of their engagement, they show a decided preference for three occupations, and become gaminghouse-keepers, victuallers, or money-lenders. In Chinese eating-houses, you would certainly get *cat* instead of *hare,* in a Chinese gaming-house you would be stript of your very shirt; and to a Chinese money-lender, you would have to pay a rate of interest which no Jew ever ventured to demand. The lowest interest they accept on loans is fifty per cent, and they not only use the articles left as pledges, but even let them on hire. One old usurer has been known to wear a pair of shoes on which he had advanced a piastre at four reales per month interest.

In a recent sitting of the legislature, when a bill was presented for organizing the importation of Chinese coolies on a large scale, a deputy, who had a great antipathy to the whole race, rose and said : "Gentlemen, why the devil does anybody want to bring amongst us more apes of that sort? they are so ugly that they will destroy the beauty of our pure race (the speaker was an Indian of the Mountains), and so corrupt that they are already refused as patients in the hospitals. If we must have foreigners, let them be whites; *but not Englishmen, because they are not Christians!* After all, it would be better to have *Bozal* negroes from Africa, for we know them well; they have been brought up with us; *they have the same religion and they speak our language.*"

Fashionable Creole Negro.

The native types are not exactly the same in all the villages of the mountains, and these again differ from the villages on the coast. The difference may be attributed in part to climatic influences. The diversity of character and customs is also very perceptible between the natives of the mountain and those of the coast, owing to the fact that the latter are nearer to, and brought into more frequent contact with, the inhabitants of the capital, which they frequently visit to sell their agricultural or manufactured products. Lima receives every year a very considerable supply of fruit, fowls, etc., from the nearer villages on the coast both north and south.

Mountaineer Indians.

The number of mountaineer Indians in Lima is very small. Of those who live there constantly, the men follow the trade of hawking ice, and the women are *fresqueras* (dealers in refreshments), nursemaids, or servants. The Indian woman of the mountains is neither very industrious nor very intelligent, and seldom learns to speak Spanish well.

Indian woman of the North coast (Huacho).

Indian woman of the South coast (Chilca).

Mountaineer Indian woman (*fresquera*).

The majority of the mountaineer Indians seen in Lima are *arrieros* (muleteers), who convey passengers and goods from one town

Indian *arrieros* (muleteers).

GENERAL MANUEL Y LA RIVANCO

Formerly Dictator of Peru

to another. As the state of the roads in Peru does not allow of using carriages, and there is no regular posting service, all who have to travel or send goods into the interior are obliged to employ the *arrieros*. The Indian, though at first sight appearing very simple and obsequious, well knows that those who seek his aid cannot travel without it, and therefore imposes his own conditions with an air of superiority. A dialogue somewhat to the following effect usually takes place between the traveller and the *arriero* :

" Have you mules for Jauja? "

" Yes, *taita* (papa). "

" What is the hire for them? "

" How many mules do you want? "

" Two for riding and three for goods."

" Well, you must give me eighteen piastres for each."

" That is too much. Will you take eight? "

" No, *taita;* forage is dear; you will give seventeen piastres and four reales.

" No ; I will give you eight piastres and a half."

Arriero loading his mule.

" You will give me seventeen."

" Nine."

" Sixteen and a half."

" Nine and a half."

" Sixteen, if you will."

" Ten. "

" Sixteen, and not less, *señor*."

" Ten and four reals."

" Come, without more words, fifteen piastres. '

" No, *señor*, I won't give above eleven."

" Agreed, *taita*, we will take them."

" And when do you start?"

" In the morning, to-morrow or the next day."

" That will do. And are your mules good ones? Those for riding must have a very easy pace."

" They are *aguelillos* (1), *taita*. You will pay for their keep also?"

" For their keep! Am I not to pay you eleven piastres for each?"

" The keep is a separate affair."

" What does it cost?"

" Two piastres for each mule."

" I will give you one."

" No, twelve reales."

" Nine."

" Ten, at least."

" Well say ten. We start to-morrow?"

" Very good, *taita*. You will also pay the watchmen on the road?"

" The watchmen?"

" The men who watch the mules while grazing."

" How much are they paid?"

" A real every night for each animal."

" I consent... Good bye, till to-morrow."

" Good bye, *taita*. You will also pay for my men's *coca* (2)."

" What again?"

" How can it be otherwise, señor?"

---

(1) The Indians give this name to a very small horse, lean-looking, but taking very short and quick steps.

(2) The *coca* is a Peruvian plant of which the Indians chew the leaves, and consider them very nourishing.

HIS EXCELLENCY FRÉDÉRIC BARREDA
Plenipotentiary of Peru at Washington (U.S)

" How much will that cost?"

" One piastre for each man."

" I will give four reals."

" Say five."

" Agreed; to-morrow morning then?"

" Yes, *taita.*"

This to-morrow morning is two or three o'clock in the afternoon, not of the following day, but of the third or fourth after the bargain.

Indian carrier making purchases.

When the *arriero* arrives at Lima he makes purchases for himself and the persons of his village. He carries a sack into which he promiscuously thrusts books, candles, drapery, etc., and throws the whole on his back. No little patience is required to deal with Indians; they haggle for every farthing, turn the goods they wish to have over and over again, go to one tradesman after another, and only decide at the very last moment.

It has been said that a bull's strength lies in its horns, and a man's in his arms: the Indian's is in his back; with a box or other

heavy load slung behind him, he will walk a long distance before
he is tired. The women are also indefatigable. They never carry their
children in their arms, and when we come to speak of the *rabonas*
(soldier's wives) we shall see that they will carry on their backs their
whole family and household goods. At Lima, and indeed in Peru

Indian woman travelling.

generally, man's strength lies : among the whites, in the shoulders;
among the negroes, in the head; among the Indians in the back.
Woman's chief power is found : among the Indians, in the feet;
among negresses, in the tongue; among the whites in the eyes.

MORAL, INTELLECTUAL, AND PHYSICAL QUALITIES
OF THE LIMANIANS.

Whatever efforts may have been made to disparage the Limanians,
there can be no doubt that they possess many estimable qualities in
a high degree. Sincerity and frankness, with generosity and disin-
terestedness, are their principal virtues. If the Limanians deserve

any particular reproach, it is that, having a predilection for good living, being always ready to oblige a friend and not less inclined to lend a helping hand to the needy, they generally live beyond their incomes. They very seldom save money, and still less frequently can they be accused of avarice. As there is no rule, however absolute, which is not liable to exceptions, the fact is certain that if prodigality be *the virtue or the defect* of the majority of the Limanians, there are many who profess the principles of economy even to stinginess.

The excellent qualities of the heart, deep-feeling, affection for a friend, and strong family attachment, are accompanied by a brilliant and ardent imagination and a subtle intellect precociously developed. If political events did not exercise in Peru a direct and nearly always disastrous influence, even in the most intimate relations of private life; if this influence did not facilitate the entrance of young men into public careers; if there were strictness and justice in the distribution of office; if, in fine, there were any stimulants for really studious men, education would not be so imperfect as it now is; men like those who, in other times, obtained such high renown in literature and science, even in Europe, would not now be so rare in Lima. As soon as a young man has obtained some kind of diploma; as soon as, trusting to his natural talents rather than to his learning, he enters the field of journalism, he fancies that he has no need of further knowledge or study : such is the principal cause which makes many of them, endowed with really superior intellect, remain all their lives superficial smatterers, though they consider themselves fit for anything.

That the natives of Lima are generally well-disposed is evident from the criminal statistics. The very few crimes committed in the capital are nearly always perpetrated by persons who come from the provinces or from foreign countries. Cases of poisoning are extremely rare; parricide and infanticide still more so. The Limanian, when excited by party-spirit or personal hatred, always shrinks, even if he meditates vengeance, from the bare idea of shedding his enemy's blood.

7

The women of Lima are undeniably among those who deserve the highest panegyrics for the natural qualities with which Providence has favoured them; gentle, amiable, and loving, they display an intelligence and imagination all the more remarkable as the education of their sex has till quite recently been altogether neglected. They are generally very quick of understanding : needlework, music, painting, dancing, are for them so easy, that but very few are destitute of these acquirements.

The natives of Lima are of middle height, scarcely any of them exceeding six Spanish feet ($5\frac{1}{2}$ feet English). Admitting the principle of those physiologists who assert that the physical development always takes place at the expense of the intellectual, the moderate stature of the Limanians would seem to confirm what has been said above. The colour of the natives, even those born of European parents, is swarthy, somewhat inclining to a yellow tint. Judging from their physiognomy, most of them appear to be sprightly, gay, and frank. Their eyes are nearly always dark or black, as is also their hair, though light hair and green or blue eyes are not uncommon. The slim figures of the Limanian ladies, their small well-shaped feet, the elegance and ease of their deportment, have always been acknowledged and extolled. Whether they are beautiful and have nothing to envy the women of other countries, the portraits contained in this book will tell better than any verbal description. These portraits are not the fantastic productions of art, but photographs taken from life.

NATIONAL COSTUME.

The national garments called the *saya y manto* (1), formerly so much used for visiting and walking, are now things of the past ; and, either through our want of taste, or because we could never discover the beauties of the *saya*, we do not regret its complete

(1) The *saya* was an upper skirt, gathered in very narrow plaits and worn over the dress. The *manto* was a kind of hood, fastened round the waist and drawn up to cover the head.

M LOUIS F. ALBERTINI
First Secretary of the legation of Peru in France

disappearance. If the pretty foot of a lady wearing it could not escape the notice of the least curious observer, the truth nevertheless compels us to say that this garment, owing to its scant proportions, masked the outlines of the figure in such a way as to deprive the wearer of all grace and elegance. Our ladies felt all the inconvenience of this narrow-plaited *saya*, when in stepping over a gutter they could not help wetting the toe of their white satin shoe, and they would have been greatly embarrassed, if compelled to run from some threatening danger. The *saya* had therefore to undergo

Veiled lady going to Mass.

a modification required both by decency and convenience : it was reduced to a kind of skirt plaited for only five or six finger-breadths at the waist. Fashion, which often runs into extravagance, then commanded that the *saya*, to be elegant and worthy to appear in places of public resort, should be nothing but fringe and ornaments, the whole richness of the toilet consisting in the costly scarf, and in the beauty and elegance of the black or white satin shoes and of the silk stockings.

The *saya* was the garment generally worn for morning visits, for going to church, for walking or following processions. In large assemblages of people, as at bull-fights, for instance, there might be seen a great number of torn *sayas* worn by the prettiest girls of Lima. The *manto* (hood) so disguised the wearer that even intimate friends could not recognize each other. It is easy to imagine that the fair Limanian took great advantage of this circumstance. The gallant who accosted her must have no little self-confidence to endure the sly repartees and biting sarcasms which escaped from the cherry-lips of a lady thus veiled. But what disappointments often

Veiled lady in a public garden.

occurred! An elegant figure, a white and well-turned arm, a tiny little foot, the corner of an expressive black eye, were not unfrequently found to belong to a toothless old hag whose other eye was wanting. The artful use of the hood has many a time drawn the unsuspecting coxcomb into the toils of an ugly and repulsive old matron; nor was this all : well-shaped negresses and *zambas*, covering their hands and arms with long silk or kid gloves reaching to the elbow, and letting the *saya* fall low enough to hide their splay feet, have ere now attracted by their slim waists, a swarm of elegant

COMMANDANT OF THE COSSACKS OF THE GUARD

dandies anxious to win by honeyed words the good graces of these sable venuses.

Ultimately the *saya* lost its sway, and that extinguisher-like head-gear called the *manto* also disappeared; but the fair Limanian, ever anxious to enhance her beauty by a little mystery, adopted in their stead the *manto chilena* (Chilian mantilla), with which she now veils and disguises herself, but less completely than with the *manto*.

Lady veiled with the Chilian mantilla.

The mantilla now, as the *saya* formerly, is worn for neighbourly visits and going to church.

The Limanian lady, spoiled from her very cradle, soon acquires a passion for rich dresses, and generally has the taste to choose such as best set off her charms. The portraits given in this book prove that the newest fashions of Paris are adopted in Lima a few weeks later.

The Limanian has a great partiality for perfumes and flowers, and she has not long lost the habit of making fragrant bouquets of orange-flowers, jasmine, etc., to present to her favourite male friends on festive occasions.

The gentlemen of Lima dress in the European fashion. A few years back, however, two or three individuals might be seen in the streets of that city, who, long after the introduction of trowsers, persisted in wearing breeches like their fathers, until death transferred them to that land where changes of fashion are unknown.

The general garment of the lower classes, especially at night, is the *poncho*, a kind of round woollen cloak, with a hole in the middle for the head, and which covers the whole person from the shoulders almost to the knees. By day, the *poncho* is worn only by persons who ride into the country on horseback, to protect their clothes from rain or dust.

Very few people wear garments peculiar to their occupations or professions. Physicians and barristers dress like all other gentlemen, though the latter when pleading before the tribunals are expected to wear all black with a dress-coat.

Soldiers, ecclesiastics, and nuns are the only persons who wear a peculiar costume. The uniforms of soldiers and sailors differ little from those seen in Europe. The same remark holds true of priests, with this difference, that in Lima they wear, over the cassock, a black cloak reaching to the middle of the leg (1), and their hat is neither round nor three-cornered, but resembles a boat in shape and is nearly two feet long. It is called a *teja* (tile).

The colour of the clothes worn by ecclesiastics varies according to their order : the friars of La Merced wear white; the Augustines, black; the Dominicans, black and white; the Franciscans, blue or gray. Their costume consists of a kind of cassock, a cloak with a hood and a sort of apron (2). The pride of the monks is an enormous black cap, very stiff, and in the form of a tower.

The Ministers of State, if civilians, wear black on all official occasions, with a blue sash and a cocked hat. The President is distinguished by a wide sash of two colours.

The chiefs of some of the Government offices have cocked hats and coats embroidered with gold on the collars and cuffs. The di-

(1) See page 29.
(2) See page 28.

plomatic agents and consuls have a uniform nearly the same as that worn by French diplomatists.

The ministers of the courts and the inferior judges wear, during official ceremonies, black coats embroidered with silk of the same colour ; the rest of their dress is also black; then they have a sword, a cane, and a cocked hat. The judges of the Supreme Court have, as a distinctive mark, a gold medal suspended from the neck by a ribbon of two colours. The ribbon of the judges in the superior courts is deep scarlet.

Mechanics and working-people in general have no particular costume.

For morning calls and walking there are no exclusive garments; but for ceremonious visits, the usage is in favour of black frock-coats and trowsers, with white waistcoats and black cravats; for very formal visits the black dress-coat is indispensable.

For friendly evening parties, the use of the frock-coat is universal; the dress-coat is only worn for grand balls, and is always accompanied by a white cravat.

For funerals, anniversary services for the dead, and visits of condolence, gentlemen wear entire suits of black with gloves of the same colour.

Ladies wear, for balls, silk dresses of light colours, and of any colour whatever for visits; entirely black toilets are only used for going to church or mourning visits. Wedding costumes are all white.

DEVOTIONS. — NUESTRO AMO.

The women of Lima are devout; they never, without good cause, miss attending the principal services of the church.

The ordinary prayers of the day are said on rising; at half-past nine in the morning, when the Cathedral bell announces the consecration of the host at high mass; at sunset, and on going to bed. The bells of all the churches are rung at eight o'clock in the evening, and devout persons then say a few prayers, which, at that hour, are believed to deliver *souls from purgatory.*

On hearing the Cathedral bells ring in the morning, and those of all the churches at sunset (the *Angelus*), all who are walking in the streets stop and take off their hats.

When *extreme unction* is carried to a person at the point of death, which is nearly always done in procession with more or less people following, men and women of all ages and conditions uncover their heads and fall on their knees, as soon as they perceive the bearers of the Holy Sacrament.

It is a common saying, and, in my opinion, well–founded, that the rich make a great noise on entering this world, a great noise during their lifetime, and a great noise for some days before they leave it (unless taken off by sudden or violent death), and the noise continues for a few days after their decease.

Nothing can be more certain than this. When a lady of high position, whether from birth or riches, approaches the solemn crisis of her interesting situation, she puts the whole house in commotion: lackeys are sent in hot haste to fetch the physician and midwife; while, of the maid-servants, some hasten to inform their *señora's* nearest relatives of her sufferings, others *to wring the fowl's neck,* to look out the cradle, childbed linen, etc.

The future mother, however exalted her social rank, suffers at that moment as intensely as the humblest of her sex, and gives way to groans and tears. At last, God grants her a happy delivery, and messengers are instantly dispatched in all directions to apprise her kindred and friends that the world counts one more unit of humanity who will one day become God knows what.

As for the poor, they make much less ado; they send few messengers to announce the birth of their offspring. Our women of the mountains give birth to their children by the wayside in the cold and desert cordilleras. The moment their children are born they wrap them, not in fine embroidered linen, but in coarse woollens, hang them at their backs and proceed on their journey.

That the rich man makes a great noise during his life is a fact which requires no demonstration : dinners, concerts, balls, horses, carriages, etc., etc., are his means of display. That a great ado is made some days before his death we have ample proof at Lima in the numerous processions which accompany the parish priest when he carries the last consolations of religion to the patient whose physician has pronounced the fatal sentence *that all human help is unavailing*.

When the procession of *Nuestro Amo* (Our Lord) leaves the parish-church, the fact is announced by ringing a small bell to summon all the *hermanos* (members of confraternities) who, from a feeling of devotion, have imposed on themselves the duty of escorting and lighting the *Santísimo* (Holy Sacrament). If the dying man be of humble condition, there are but few attendants with very small lanterns, and not more than two or three chanters; but if he belong to the upper class, in addition to a great number of friends

Alumbrante (lantern-bearer) accompanying the viaticum.

who, taper in hand, join the procession, *los alumbrantes* (lantern-bearers) of the parish come in great force, dressed in flaming-red cloaks, and carrying large ornamental lanterns; there are also *za-humadoras*(1), and a military band completes the cortege. Passengers and idlers join the procession, some because they wish to be thought friends of the *viajero* (traveller starting for the other world), and others because they have nothing better to do. With such parade as this the devout Limanian departs this life, and, like the faithful elsewhere, never leaves its pomps and vanities till they leave him.

In all the parishes there are *Cofradías del Santísimo* (brotherhoods of the Most Holy Sacrament), who take charge of the worship of *Nuestro Amo* and are careful that lights shall never be wanting. These brotherhoods have revenues, but as *store is no sore*, they collect alms in various ways. Often a negro or a devout *zambo* parades the streets crying : ¡ *Para la cera de Nuestro Amo!* (for Our Lord's

¡ *Para la cera de Nuestro Amo!* (For the tapers of our Lord!)

tapers!) The street-boys of Lima, like those of all other large cities, have no great faith in the probity of devotees, and they shout

(1) The *zahumadoras* are women who carry small chafing-dishes on which they burn incense and other perfumes.

in reply: *La mitad para mi, la mitad para el Amo* (half for me, half for the Lord).

No one can imagine the ardent zeal of the sanctimonious female devotees of the different parishes; those who belong to one will insist that their *Nuestro Amo* is much better than any of the others can boast; they assert that their own is richer and more splendidly served than all the rest. The splendour consists more especially in the canopy, the number of ornaments, and the large size of the lanterns.

RELIGIOUS FESTIVALS.

Within the last few years the number of religious festivals and processions has considerably diminished, but the most remarkable change is the decline in the magnificence and splendour of the latter. The ceremonies of the Holy Week are but the more shadow of what they once were, and scarcely a reminiscence remains of the gorgeous display made by the Friars of La Merced, on Good Friday when the procession of the *Santo Sepulcro* used to start from their church.

Having touched on this subject, we will give a concise account of what these ceremonies used to be and of what they are now.

In bygone times, as at present, during the week following Passion Sunday, it was customary for priests to issue from the churches accompanied by two pages in livery, one of whom carried a huge parasol and the other a large salver, formerly of silver, but now of any less costly metal. The priests went from door to door collecting money for the *Santo Monumento*. On Palm Sunday the palms were blessed in the church, and in the afternoon the procession of the *Borriquito* (ass's colt) left the Chapel of the Baratillo in memory of Christ's triumphal entry into Jerusalem. The procession is still kept up, but without the numerous following and splendour of former times. The *borriquito* or rather *borriquita* (ass's filly) used at Lima is a wooden one; but in some villages the Saviour is carried by a she-ass. The history of *Las Burras del Señor* (the Lord's she-asses)

at Chorrillos , is well known. The first ass employed for the pro—
cession, many long years ago, naturally became an object of vene—
ration for the Indians, who not only allowed it to remain at liberty
and unworked, but also fed it well. Rest and abundant food had
made the animal very fat. It had the free range of the village and
the neighbouring valleys, but on Palm Sunday it spontaneously went

¡ Para el Santo Monumento! (¡For the *Santo Monumento!*)

to the church accompanied by its young one. The race of this sa—
gacious ass is not extinct; its descendants still perform the same
services and enjoy the same privileges and attentions as their prede—
cessors. It is said that, down to the present time, there has been no
instance of the ass having failed in attendance or of its having come
without a foal.

On Maundy Thursday and Good Friday, in the morning, the ser—
vice of the Passion was celebrated in all the churches. The crowds
which then flocked to the churches of *La Merced* and of *San Agus-*

tin, and in the evening to the *Tenebræ* at the latter, were really extraordinary. On Maundy Thursday the monuments of the Passion were uncovered in all the churches. The finest and most famous was that of *San Francisco* representing the *Last Supper.* This monument drew the most visitors, not so much from any feeling of devotion as to see the apostle Judas Iscariot with a face redder than fire and with a Chili pepper-pod in his mouth. To judge the health of the apostles by their faces, Judas, who was of a sanguine temperament, appeared in more robust health than his companions.

The procession which started from *San Agustin,* on Maundy Thursday, presented a finer show of statues than those of all the other parish churches of Lima. Each group represented one of the scenes of the Passion of the Saviour. The Jews were personated by wooden images, of the natural size, to which religious zeal had attempted to give the most repulsive and ludicrous aspect possible. The statuaries could not conceive the possibility of a Jew being pale or having a human appearance : all the images consequently had such countenances as are usually attributed to demons. The people were in ecstasies at the sight of these groups, and in their enthusiasm, apostrophized the images as if they had been the living executioners who insulted and crucified the Divine Redeemer.

On Good Friday, the procession of the *San Sepulcro* used to leave the church of La Merced. Nothing could equal the rich display of chasubles, choir cloaks, and other ornaments made by these holy fathers. This procession, which might fairly be called that of the aristocracy, was followed by the most beautiful *señoras* and the richest *caballeros* of Lima.

The church of *San Pedro* also had its day. On Holy Saturday it was filled with a brilliant crowd to attend the *Gloria* mass. The night following was the *noche buena* (good night); the grocers burned Judas at twelve o'clock, the hour for the sumptuous suppers which announced the end of Lent and the beginning of the joyous feast of Easter.

All these festivals, except the processions of Maundy Thursday and Good Friday are still kept, though with less solemnity and splendour.

The grandest processions of the present day are those of *Nuestra Señora de las Mercedes* (Our Lady of Mercies), patroness of the arms of the Republic; of *Santa Rosa,* patroness of Lima; of Our Lady of the Rosary, of *Corpus Christi,* of Quasimodo, and of the *Señor de los Milagros* (Our Lord of Miracles).

Few saints, male or female, had more votaries at Lima than *Nuestra Señora del Rosario.* There were divers brotherhoods devoted to her worship, each making a different addition to her name: one called her *Nuestra Señora del Rosario de los Negros* (of the Negroes), another *de los Pardos* (of the Mulattoes), a third *de los Indios* (of the Indians), and a fourth *de los Blancos* (of the Whites). These *castes* rivalled each other in decorating their Virgin for the annual processions, all of which are now reduced to one. We know not whether this change is owing to the fact that the brethren of different colours have recently become convinced that there is only one Virgin, and but one God for all the races of mankind, or because the Mulattoes and Indians are less religious than they used to be. We say nothing of the negroes, as their brotherhood has naturally ceased to exist owing to their almost total extinction. As already stated, the procession of *Nuestra Señora de los Negros,* on Corpus Christi-day, used to be followed by troops of negroes disguised as demons.

On the festival of Quasimodo (the Sunday after Easter), the procession of *Nuestro Amo* starts from all the parish-churches and chapels of ease. On no day of the year do the streets of Lima present a more animated appearance. The first procession leaves the *Sagrario* before six in the morning, the streets having been previously watered and strewed with flowers. The ladies are already in their balconies, from which they scatter perfumes when *El Santisimo* passes before them. As the processions of all the parish-churches set off at different hours, the streets are filled with them till three or four in the afternoon. On this occasion, *Nuestro Amo* visits all convalescent patients who desire the consolation of receiving him.

A few years back the *Quasimodo* processions, as well as those of

Corpus Christi were followed by bands of mummers dressed to imitate demons, while others not less hideous and ridiculous, appeared as *Giants* and *Papa-huevos*. The former were colossal pasteboard

Giants and Papa-huevos.

images, carried by a negro concealed inside, and the latter were boys wearing masks in the shape of a head which covered all their body but the legs.

However, while the country was still a Spanish colony, many persons protested against these exhibitions, which, under the pretext of honouring the Divinity, were offensive to public morality, and turned religion itself into ridicule; but the abuse was tolerated, and we may even say authorized, by the viceroys, for they took no steps to put an end to the barbarous practices introduced by their predecessors.

Among the curious documents handed down from those good old times, we find a petition, addressed to the government of Lima by the priest of a parish in the capital, against a decree issued in 1817 forbidding the presence of giants in the *Quasimodo* processions. The worthy priest propounds his complaint as follows :

" Most Excellent Señor. — The priest N. N., Doctor of Sacred Theology, of the most illustrious Royal and Pontifical University of San Marcos, incumbent of the parish of... has the honour respectfully to represent to your Excellency : that it is a notorious wrong and a manifest offence against the majesty of the Divine Pastor, Redeemer, and Saviour of all generations to have forbidden this year, by *paramount* but not competent authority, the presence of devils and giants in the public processions of *Quasimodo* (Sunday next). The measure is unreasonable and unnecessary, 1. because *the said devils form an innocent escort* to the Divine Majesty, and the people delight to see them prostrate themselves before God ; and 2., because the giants, without frightening children, attract a more numerous crowd of devout persons, but for whose presence the Divine procession would be completely deserted. Your petitioner therefore begs of your Excellency and of your pious heart, that from my church of..... my faithful parishioners may proceed disguised as devils and giants; I await this favour from your pious Christian heart.

"† Dr. N. N. *Cura de*...

" I further pray that there may be *Papa-huevos.* "

The viceroy, moved by so much eloquence and convinced by the reverend theologian's arguments, replied in these terms :

" In conformity with the prayer of this petition, the venerable *cura* of... is permitted to have four giants to accompany the Divine Majesty on Quasimodo Sunday next, and also *Papa-huevos.* (Signed). "

The procession of the *Señor de los Milagros* (Lord of Miracles), called the *Rodeo de las Viejas* (procession of old women), though many young girls join it, starts from the church of the Nazarene nuns on the 18th of October, in commemoration of one of the earthquakes which destroyed the capital. The *Señor de los Milagros* has been made the patron of earthquakes, for the reasons given in the following popular legend.

" At a certain place in Lima called *Pachacamilla,* there stood a building used as a place of meeting by the *Angolas* negroes, one of whom painted on the wall a picture of Christ on the Cross. On the 13th of November 1655, a violent earthquake, which destroyed a great number of houses, threw down all those of Pachacamilla and the walls of the negroes' assembly-room, except the one on which the crucifixion was painted. The standing wall was preserved, and the other three walls were rebuilt, but the place was some time afterwards transferred to other owners, who, wishing to efface the picture, covered it over with lime-wash and paint, but all their efforts were vain, for it only looked brighter and fresher. A miracle so astounding induced a man named Andrés Leon to erect on the spot, in 1670, a thatched house to shelter the persons who went to pray before the crucifix. Subsequently, Captain Don Sebastian de Antuñano bought the place along with the surrounding property, and the church of the Nazarene nuns was built on the spot. The picture of the Lord of Miracles still exists on the wall behind the high-altar."

The *Señor de los Milagros* is followed on procession days by individuals who call themselves *penitents,* but their only claim to that character is the absurd disguise which they assume. These men solicit alms from the public, crying with a loud voice : " Help us to buy tapers for *Nuestro Amo* and the *Señor de los Milagros!* — Where are the devotees of last year? "

This procession continues two days, and the *old women,* in relating what churches it is to enter, say : " *El Señor,* on the day he goes out, eats in the church of the Conception, sleeps in that of the *Descalzas* (Barefooted nuns); on the second day, he eats at St. Catherine's and sleeps at home. "

There is no regular procession without two sorts of attendants, the *mistureras* and the *zahumadoras.* The *señoras* dress the young negresses and *zambas* in their service with all possible richness and elegance; those who are to accompany the procession are splendidly

8

Penitent.

Misturera.

decked out that day with costly scarfs, gold rings, clasps, and ear-pendants set with diamonds.

The *mistureras* have on their heads large salvers holding flowers, and the *zahumadoras* carry in their hands silver chafing-dishes,

Zahumadora.

filled with live coals, on which they burn a very fragrant resin called *zahumerio*.

At the hour of vespers on certain important festivals, like that

Buñuelera (fritter-woman).

of *Nuestra Señora de las Mercedes*, there may be seen in the streets near the church women selling *picantes* (highly-spiced viands), fritters, and *chicha morada* (an intoxicating beverage made from Indian corn). We do not know the origin of this custom; but what we do know of these open-air kitchens is, that the disagreeable odour they diffuse, and the obstacles they place in the way of passengers, cannot in any way contribute to the solemnity of a religious festival.

The crosses erected in the cemeteries of the parish churches are taken down in the month of May to be repainted and embellished. Not long since, it was the custom, on the day of restoring them to their places, to celebrate the famous spectacles of the *Moors and Christians*.

Two large stages were erected in the middle of the streets nearest the churches. On one of these figured the Moorish army with the king at its head; on the other the Christian host, also with its king.

From each camp issued ambassadors on horseback to defy the hostile monarch, and delivered burlesque tirades in the rude and uncouth language of the populace. When we remember that the actors in these farces were negro water-carriers, it will be easy to conceive *all the merit* of the tragic declamation required by the subject.

Nothing could well be more unsightly than the aspect of the streets full of a rabble excited by ample libations of spirituous liquors. The side-walks were covered with benches, tables, and counters, on which were placed chairs for the spectators; the ludicrous farces of these negro monarchs parodying the kings of Granada; the numerous liquor-sellers, and the fritter-women whose fires filled the streets with smoke, were anything but ornamental or proofs of the civilization of the people.

VISITS AND PARTIES.

The families of Lima have no particular days or hours for receiving visitors. Friends of either sex are welcomed at any hour, except, of course, early in the morning, and at meal-times.

Visits to persons not intimately known are generally made on week–days, from one till four in the afternoon, or from seven till eleven in the evening. The *señoras* are very amiable and courteous, and use every means compatible with propriety and good-breeding to set their visitors at ease. To be a foreigner is considered a claim on the kindness of persons of good society, just as much as it is a ground for mockery on the part of the. populace. The men of the lower classes look on all foreigners as Jews, and the women call them *brutes,* simply because they are generally unable to speak Spanish.·

Formerly it was the custom to offer visitors different kinds of refreshments according to the hour at which they arrived : from noon till four o'clock they were requested to take *las once* (1), and in the evening chocolate, biscuits, etc. At present, tea is generally given, which causes people who have passed their fiftieth year to say that the English, with their insipid slops, have brought stinginess into fashion.

In bygone times nearly all ladies smoked, so that the first thing they offered to their friends was a cigar, then perfumes, flowers, etc. This practice has also disappeared, without the English having re-placed it by another.

Great evening parties and balls are very rare, a fact which would not seem to say much for our sociability. On certain days of the year, the members and intimate friends of families do indeed meet; but those ceremonious invitations which afford such excellent opportunities for easily acquiring polite manners and for drawing closer the bonds of friendship are, we repeat, extremely rare; and yet the young ladies of Lima are enthusiastically fond of dancing and music, and there are very few of them who cannot play the piano and also sing a little.

(1) *Las once* (the eleven) consisted generally of bread, cheese, fruit, olives, *aguardiente* (brandy); from the eleven letters of this word came the expression *las once,* a euphemism which was substituted for the unaristocratic phrase : ¡ *Vamos á echar un trajo!* (Let us have a drink!)

FELICITATIONS, COMPLIMENTS OF CONDOLENCE, ETC.

Spanish courtesy, of which we still retain some remains (and God forbid that we should ever lose them to accept in their stead a false and hollow politeness), was once proverbial throughout the world. The frankness, high-breeding, and generosity of our ancestors were accompanied by a strict etiquette, which made them regard as a breach of politeness and friendship the omission to congratulate a friend on any accession of fortune or to condole with him in his reverses and sufferings.

It was the usage to visit a more or less intimate friend, on his obtaining office; when he returned from a journey previous to which he had taken leave of you ; on his marriage; on his birth-day; when a child was born to him, and in general on any occurrence which could cause him joy or grief.

A gentleman about to marry always announces the event to his friends; the ancient formula for such letters was nearly in these terms : *Don N. N. announces to you his marriage with Donna N. N. and both place themselves at your disposal.* Etiquette required that the persons receiving these letters should pay a visit to the newly married couple and express the wish that their happiness might endure for *many centuries and that God would send them plenty of hildren.* According to present usage, nothing more is sent than a card bearing the names of the parties; in the highest circles emblems are seldom added, but the names are sometimes placed in the middle of a ring formed of a ribbon tied in a true-lovers' knot and hanging from the beak of a bird.

The compliments addressed to any person on his or her birthday, were limited to saying : *May you pass many happy days in the society of your honourable family!* and the reply was : *May it also be in your company!* The compliment is now suppressed, and cards are sent instead.

On the birth of a child, the parents usually send a message by a servant, who, no great while since, when slavery still existed, used to say : *My senorita wishes her ladyship many happy days, hopes that her ladyship is well, and informs her ladyship that she has another servant at her command.* This message would give rise to a dialogue like the following:

"Ah! she has been confined?"

"Yes, *mi amita* (my little mistress)."

"And of what?"

"Of a boy, *señorita.*"

"At what o' clock?"

"Eleven last night, *señorita.*"

"Who attended her?"

"*Mi amita Joaquina.*"

"And when will the christening be?"

"This evening, *señorita.*"

"And who is to be the godfather?"

"*Mi amo* (my master), Señor Don Antuco."

"Well, tell your *señorita* that I thank God she has been happily delivered, and that I will see her this evening with the *niñas* (little girls)."

"Adieu then, *mi amita.*"

As to the ancient and modern modes of paying compliments of condolence, the reader is referred to what has been said on mourning and funerals.

Modern refinement has put an end to the *plácemes*, stupid compliments formerly paid to parents who had lost a child of tender age. In the certainty that such innocent creatures have not to undergo the pains of Purgatory, but that they go straight to the presence of God, it was customary to say to the mother: *May God grant you life and health to send angels to heaven!* which was equivalent to wishing her the affliction of losing more children. This compliment, as we have said, has fallen into desuetude, and none now express wishes that their friends may send inhabitants to heaven.

Congratulations of neighbourhood are offered by the persons living in a quarter to those who come to reside near them. They consist in assuring the new-comer that he or she is welcome, and in offering any services that may be required. This visit is returned on the following day. The person who offered the congratulations calls again in a week, and after that visit has been returned, the parties either become intimate or all relations cease between them.

BESA-MANOS (KISSING OF HANDS).

The grand official receptions which used to be held on the anniversaries of the Independence and of the famous battle of Ayacucho have fortunately ceased.

The President, the authorities, and the corporations used to attend (as they do still) a thanksgiving mass at the Cathedral, in commemoration of those great events. After the religious service, the authorities accompanied the President back to his palace, where he took his stand under a canopy in the reception-room, to hear harangues addressed to him by the heads of the corporations and the professors or students of the national colleges. All these speeches turned on the inevitable themes of "thanking the Almighty for the blessing of Independence, of deploring the political misfortunes of the past year and of anticipating the happiness promised by the present." In these pompous declamations there were incessant allusions to *Mars and his ravages, Minerva and her benefits, the olive-branch of peace, the torch of discord, the lion of Iberia, the yoke of conquest, the three centuries,* and all the phraseology invented about half a century ago, and repeated by *patriots* ever since.

It was usual to conclude with these or similar words: *May Peru be happy! May the tree of liberty yield us rich and abundant fruit under the wise, just, and illustrious government of your Excellency! Such are the wishes of the Court of Accounts* (or of the illustrious University of San Marcos) *in whose name I have the honour to congratulate your Excellency on this day,* ever memorable for our country. I have said."

The President, whether an orator or not, would then reply to these eloquent or impertinent harangues, by offering his arm, his sword, and all his faculties, to secure the happiness of Peru during the following year; after which, everybody would withdraw, commenting on the merits of the different speakers and laughing at the ill-luck or incapacity of those who had broken down in the midst of their speeches.

After the abolition of this ceremonial, a proceeding was adopted, less ridiculous and attended with positive advantages for the adorers of the Independence. The Government now invites to the palace the *veterans* of the year 20 and those of the current year; and sets before them a table abundantly provided with viands and wine (1). The veterans enjoy themselves and make speeches, thanking God that, through the Independence and the progress of industry, they can now drink

Aquellos vinos puros,
Generosos, maduros,
Gustosos y fragantes,
Que no tomaban ántes (2),

that is, in those glorious times when they were fighting for the liberty of Peru.

NATIONAL REPASTS.

Though the influence of foreigners, among whom may be mentioned some few high priests of the culinary temple, has led to the disappearance of some creole dishes from the dinner and supper table, there still remain many which will never be abandoned by those whose fortune precludes the use of foreign delicacies.

First on the list of national dishes stands the *puchero,* to which, if popular traditions may be believed, the monks of Lima were indebted for the rotundity of their venerable persons. The Limanian *puchero* is, in fact, a dish which, from the variety and succulence

(1) If it so happens that they are not overthrown by some recently victorious revolutionist.

(2) Those wines, pure, rich, and ripe, of exquisite flavour and fragrance, which they rarely drank before.

of its constituent principles, forms a good meal of itself alone. To make a *puchero,* according to the strict gastronomic rules, put into a kettle a large piece of beef or mutton, some cabbage, sweet potatoes, salt pork, sausage meat, pig's feet, yucas (1), bananas, quinces, peas, and rice, with annotto and salt for seasoning. Add a sufficient quantity of water and let the whole stew gently for five or six hours, then serve in a tureen or deep dish. It is easy to conceive that whoever eats heartily of this heterogeneous compound will not be in any danger of dying from inanition for the next twelve hours.

Another national dish is the *chupe,* which, though less esteemed than the *puchero,* is, nevertheless very relishing. It consists of potatoes boiled in water or milk, to which are added fresh-water crabs, fried fish, eggs, cheese, lard, and salt. The secret of making a *chupe* in perfection is said to be known to the cooks of Lima only.

The *carapulca,* the *locro,* the *quinua atamalada,* etc. are the daily food of the poorer inhabitants of Peru.

The favourite dainties for Sunday breakfasts are : the *chicharron,* which is nothing but pork fried in lard; the *tamal,* a paste made of maize flour and lard, in which pistachioes, pimento, and slices of pork are enclosed, then wrapped in green plantain leaves and grilled over the fire; the *pastilillo,* made of yuca meal, which is fried and eaten with sugar.

For dinner parties, the French fashion is followed, that being preferred as far as concerns repasts. The tables are richly ornamented, and the service is effected in good style. The pressing entreaties by which the master of the house used to show his respect for the guests have fallen into desuetude. No one now ever hears at table such annoying expressions as : *Jesus! how little you eat! shall I offer you another slice? Take some of this; it is excellent; try this dish; it was made by Fulanita* (2), and other similar appeals, which

(1) *Yuca,* Adam's needle, a long round root, very white and mealy.

(2) This *Fulanita* (Spanish for *So-and-so*) was the mistress of the house or one of her daughters.

often induced the visitor to eat in spite of himself, and without relish, under pain of being thought ill-bred.

It is scarcely necessary to say that the grand banquets of former times were composed of all the favourite dishes of the day. The bill of fare of a great dinner would be something like the following : *Sopa teologa* (parson's soup); *puchero; duck en querregue* (with melted butter); *stuffed turkey; roast fowls; forced meat balls; carapulca; almendrado* (meat with almond sauce); *pigeons;* and eight or ten other items; for the dessert, there was a great variety of fruit and sweets, among which always appeared *la leche asada* (literally, roasted milk, a kind of clotted cream), and the *maná* (yolks of eggs); the last article, without which the dinner would have been thought incomplete, was the traditional *empanada* (1). The sumptuousness of the banquet was estimated by the cost of the *empanada*. This cake, made by pastry-cooks, was always in the shape of an oblong rectangle. There have been *empanadas* so large that two men were required to bring them to table. The *empanada* was always received with cheers and every demonstration of joy.

The wine generally drunk during the dinner was Frontignac ; Champagne was brought with the dessert; but many persons preferred *Pisco* or *Italia* (2).

Toasts were regarded as indispensable : the guests always drank each others' healths, and he who proposed the toast made a speech which invariably concluded with the panegyric of the host or the members of his family. The speakers were always loudly applauded, the whole company crying, as each resumed his seat : *Viva! viva!* at the same time striking the plates and glasses with their knives, sometimes inflicting no trifling pecuniary loss on their entertainers.

Besides toasts, one of the modes by which the company manifested *their affection* was the *bocadito* (little mouthful) : every gentleman and lady took up a piece of meat, fowl, pastry, etc., on the forks they were using, and handed the same to their neighbour, who re-

(1) The *empanada* was a sort of very large marchpane.
(2) Brandy.

turned the compliment by handing back a similar piece on his or her own fork.

Such was the profusion at all these formal dinners, that if there were only ten guests, sufficient would be prepared for thirty. I cannot call to mind the name of the shrewd individual who used to say that when a man was invited to dinner, he ought to *eat abundantly and also to carry something home.* This principle was professed at Lima thirty years ago by all classes of society. If a guest had not taken his family with him, and his house was at no great distance, he would fill a large plate from one of the dishes which he preferred and send it to his wife, with a message that *he sent her that bocadito because it had stuck in his throat;* and truly such a mouthful would have been almost enough to choke a whale. It was so generally the practice never to go home empty-handed, that a man was certain his wife and children would not fail to ask on his return : *What have you brought from the dinner?*

On the day after such a feast, the lady of the house would divide among her friends the remainder of the preserves, confectionery, and fruit, not forgetting to send a piece of the *empanada* at the same time.

For a whole fortnight afterwards, the banquet would be the subject of endless comments. Let us hear two persons of the fair sex thus indulge the charitable custom of backbiting.

" Did you go, niña (little girl), to Donna Dominguita's dinner?"

" Yes, *hija* (daughter), and would to God I had not gone!"

" Why? Was it not well served?"

" Only so-so. Just fancy that I there met Donna Josefa..."

"Which?... the wife of the treasurer of the *cofradias?*"

" Herself. If you had but seen now proud she was of her diamond *chupetes* (1)!"

" Ha-ha! only think of that! Just as if her godmother Bartola

(1) The day after the dinner was called *corcoba* (bump).
(2) Ear-pendants in the shape of almonds very much like those now worn, but larger.

were not still living; a *mestiza* (mixed breed) who was once house-
keeper in the establishment of my godfather, the Marquis of..."

" But as soon as she got married to Don Pedrito..."

" And who is this Don Pedrito? Do we know him? — Who else
was there?"

" Only a few nobodies. There was the friar N... (1)."

" Him of La Merced?"

" No, his brother, the Dominican."

" You must know that he pleased me very much. He is very
lively... *He proposed a toast in verse* and paid very high compliments
to Donna Merceditas."

" Mere flattery, *niña*, because he dined at the house..."

" There was also Dr. J... Are you aware that he is a *Zambo, very
free and easy?* He talked so much nonsense to my cousin Antuquita,
who is still *such an innocent creature* that I was obliged to keep her
close by my side."

" And how was the dinner?"

" How would you have it? Don't you know Donna Dominguita,
who is covetousness personified?"

" Her husband is more generous, but she has him under her
thumb. She manages every thing, and the *poor goose* lets her do as
she likes. Just fancy that the *Zamba* Juliana did the cooking... She
refused to engage Monte Blanco or Serapio (2) because they asked
half an *onza*. They did not get their empanada from the pastry
cook's shop at *La Merced* but from the one at *San Andrés*."

" And yet what grand airs they give themselves!"

" Grand airs, *niña*. — They even kept the fragments!"

And in this charitable style all the company were passed in re-
view.

The more peculiarly national viands are the *picantes* (spiced
dishes) which the populace especially favour, but not they alone.
The *picantes* are poison rather than food, on account of the immense proportion of pimento they contain. For some enthusiasts,

(1) Wherever there was a dinner monks would be sure to attend.
(2) Negro cooks, very famous in their day.

the most delicious ragout is that which makes them suffer most
while eating it. There are persons from whom the burning properties
of pimento draw tears, but who nevertheless smack their lips as if
they liked it beyond measure. It must be owned that a pleasure
which causes so much suffering is not over agreeable.

The *picantes* are made of fresh meat, fish, salt meat, potatoes, etc.;
but the most biting *picante,* that which oftenest compels tears, is
the *seviche.* It is composed of small pieces of fish or crabs, soaked
in the juice of bitter oranges with plenty of pimento and salt. After
lying for some hours till the fish is thoroughly impregnated with

Indian picantera.

pimento, and cooked, as it were, by its burning effect and the
acidity of the orange-juice, it is ready for the table. Whoever in-
dulges in the pleasure of eating *seviche* is sure afterwards to have
the satisfaction of passing a few moments with open mouth, and
suffering, at the very least, great irritation of the bowels.

To mitigate the burning heat caused by pimento, the people drink *chicha* (beer made of maize). Pimento employed as a condiment in small quantities is nevertheless agreeable, and produces no perceptible bad effects.

The *picantes* are sold at Lima by negresses who walk about the streets carrying their pans in a large basket on their heads, and in the low eating-houses called *picanterías*. These establishments are nearly all kept by Indian women from the mountains or the coast, some of whom have a great reputation for skill in preparing the dish.

The practise of going to *picar* (1) in these *picanterías*, on returning from the bull-fights, has ceased for some years past.

NATIONAL BEVERAGES.

The three principal beverages made in Peru and consumed at Lima are *aguardiente* (brandy), *chicha*, and *guarapo*. Wealthy persons have, however, always kept a stock of foreign wines in their cellars. At the present time, the most famous wines are familiar to all persons in easy circumstances. In some districts of the southern coast, wines are grown which have acquired great reputation even in European markets. The pure spirit of the grape has given some celebrity to the valley of *Pisco*, where it is distilled, and this was the beverage always offered at *las once* (1). This beverage is now little used by respectable persons. *Guarapo*, produced by the fermentation of cane-trash after the sugar has been extracted, was the favourite drink of the negroes, especially of the *bozales*. A distinction must be made between the mild *guarapito* intended for the negro *fair sex*, and the *achichadito*, which, on account of its strength, was preferred by the rougher sex of the same colour. *Chicha* has the pre-eminence as the national beverage; the Indians used it even under the empire of the *Incas*. *Chicha* is made of a sort of maize which is kept moist till it sprouts, and in that state it is called *jora*; it is then ground, and boiled in large kettles filled with

(1) *Picar*, to eat *picante*.
(2) See note, p. 117.

water. The decoction is afterwards allowed to ferment, and as soon
as this action ceases, the *chicha* is ready for use. In some of the
mountain districts, the *jora* is chewed instead of being ground. A
number of persons of both sexes, generally old, sit round in a ring
in the middle of which is laid the maize to be operated on. Each
person chews the corn by small handfuls and afterwards lays it to
dry, previously to being boiled, as above stated. Some persons insist that the *chicha* prepared from *jora* thus chewed is better than
that from ground *jora;* and when the filthiness of the proceeding is
objected, they reply that fire is an efficacious purifier.

    Chicha is the drink preferred by the Indians of the mountains and
the coast; but they nevertheless have a great liking for spirits.

Ecstasy produced by *chicha.*

    Chicha, as already remarked, relieves the burning heat caused by
pimento. All who like the *picantes* are also fond of *chicha,* which,
though not alcoholic, still produces a certain derangement affecting the senses and the reason.

MOURNING, FUNERALS, AND ANNIVERSARY SERVICES.

Nothing certainly could be more wearisome than the old ceremonial practised for mourning, funerals, and anniversary services.
Not only were they encumbered with an etiquette in the highest
degree ridiculous, but it might truly be said that, under the lugu-
brious appearance of a grief more or less feigned, the very memory
of the dead was outraged in whose honour so much weeping and
wailing was performed.

We will not go back to the epoch when a funeral procession was
composed of a crowd of monks, numerous friends and acquaintances, and a long string of idlers, who, taper in hand, accompanied the deceased to the church where the service was to be
performed. We will not reveal the animated conversations in which
friends and *strangers* retraced the *life* and the *miracles* of the
departed in order to lavish on him praise or reproaches which always concluded with these compassionate phrases : *May God pardon
him! He is dead at last, poor man!* Nor will we detail the scenes
which occurred during the breakfasts and *las once* (1), where the
weeping family awaited the persons invited to funerals and the services at the first anniversary of the death. After beginning to eat
with a countenance full of sorrow, and, for form's sake, heaving
sighs which did not come from the heart, they pretended to drown
their grief in repeated draughts of good liquor, then rose from
table, after having totally forgotten the virtues of the departed whose
loss they had deplored.

We will begin nearer to our own times, and relate the funeral ceremonies which were performed before black-bordered cards had realized amongst us their work of reform, propriety, and civilization.

On the second evening after the death, the corpse was removed,
as it still is, to the church, followed in silence by the friends and
most intimate acquaintances of the deceased. On the following
day, the funeral service was performed between ten and eleven in

(1) See note, p. 117.

the morning. At its close, the chief mourners, who, during the ceremony, occupied the first places on the left, nearest the coffin,
took their stand at the church door as the procession passed out,
and then proceeded in carriages with some few friends to the cemetery, while the rest of the attendants went back to the house of the
deceased and there awaited the return of the former.

The wife and other women of the family also waited this return,
assembled in a darkened room, in company with their female relatives and friends. When the mourners came back from the cemetery,
the nearest relative entered the drawing-room and opened one or
two of the windows. Then the sepulchral silence which had reigned
for three or four hours was broken, but all the conversation was in
a low and scarcely audible whisper.

The mourning continued for a month; all the friends and connections deemed it their bounden duty to keep company with the
afflicted family. The men remained in the ante-chamber, where
conversation was permitted, but in a low voice; the women, all in
deep mourning, sat in the drawing-room, gloomily lighted by the
faint glimmer of a lamp covered with crape. The only sounds heard
amongst them were sighs or doleful exclamations more or less affected; the widow or the mother wept and moaned, and it was the
duty of the attendants to utter brief interjections of *oh! oh! ah! ah!*
and make a noise as if they were diligently using their handkerchiefs. At eight in the evening the company separated. This was a
critical and painful moment for the women; some one of them
must be the first to break through the restraint of this silence and
feigned grief, to salute the rest and retire, and she who had the
courage to do this was called the *chiavata* (she-goat). It was therefore very common to hear the remark : *In the mourning for Donna
So-and-so, Donna N. N. was the chiavata.*

At present, though the religious ceremonies are performed in
the same order, people are not expected to visit the family on the
day of the funeral; acquaintances merely leave a card, while relatives and intimate friends are received without any wearisome formalities, and, all absurd manifestations of sorrow being suppressed,

there is naturally greater sincerity in the language of sympathy and consolation addressed to the bereaved.

The service for the repose of the soul of the deceased, celebrated on the first anniversary of death, consists of a mass which friends are invited to attend. It is usual to address invitations not only to one's connections but to all persons of note in the capital. As these letters request the attendance of the parties and of their friends also, the number of persons present depends much on the social position of the deceased. Some years since, the usage was for the persons inviting to take their stand at the church door after the service and shake hands with each of the invited as they retired. This ceremony, which was very tedious for all concerned, has fallen into disuse ; and the invitations for such occasions now end with the phrase : *The mourning will terminate without etiquette.*

The funerals of very young children used to be, and still are, festive solemnities.

Nothing can be more repugnant to the feelings of a parent than the custom, which may almost be called barbarous, of rejoicing over the death of a child. Civilization has already abolished this usage among the educated classes, but it still subsists among the lower orders, especially the Indians.

When a child died, its body was dressed in the costume supposed to be worn by angels, including the palm and crown ; it was then put into a coffin lined with some gay colour, strewed over with flowers, and placed on a temporary altar. At night there was a wake with music, to which the friends of the family were invited. At midnight a supper was served for all present. Among the viands, was one regarded as indispensable; this was the *salpicon,* consisting of meat and lettuces minced up together. On the morrow, the body was taken to the church where a musical mass was sung. At one time children were nearly always interred in convents of nuns.

Though the religious service still continues the same, there is no longer any wake, or altar, or *salpicon;* people have ceased to rejoice over the loss of their children, which is doubtless a gratifying symptom of our social amelioration.

JOURNALS.

No people with any pretensions to civilization can now dispense with that important element of social life called a *newspaper*. Yet Lima, with its hundred thousand inhabitants, cannot support two daily papers. Since the first publication of the *Comercio*, which has attained the respectable age of twenty-one years, many other journals have appeared, but have nearly all died in their early infancy. The *Comercio* alone suffices for all the requirements of Lima : it records the commercial movement of the capital, inserts all kinds of advertisements, publishes foreign news, opens its columns to political writers, and above all, *enlivens its miscellaneous intelligence with a good sprinkling of personalities*. Its pages offer an arena in which the young writers of the day gather their first laurels ; prose or verse, or what is neither one nor the other, there finds a refuge. The *Comercio* already forms a collection containing the political, military, literary, and general history of nearly all Peru, as well as a rather extensive scandalous chronicle of private life.

For the great majority of its readers, the chief merit of the *Comercio* lies in its numerous *comunicados* (1). When these are few or tamely written, the *Comercio* presents no interest.

Journals exclusively devoted to science or literature soon cease to appear from want of readers; but the people have a decided taste for satirical or aggressive writings, especially if they relate to politics or attack the Government. On the other hand, it is certain that these flowers have their thorns, and that if the journal is well received, its editor is in danger of losing his liberty.

NECROLOGY.

No man is wicked after death is a truth that cannot be disputed, because death deprives men of the power of doing evil; but this cause is not the only one. Very few depart this life without leaving

(1) The name given to all articles of local interest not written by the editors.

behind some one who loved them; and even he who has not had the happiness to find much affection during life, may, by means of a well-ordered will, lay the foundations of a brilliant posthumous reputation. In all parts of the world, grave-stones may be quoted in support of this assertion. No tomb has ever borne an inscription enumerating the vices or defects of its occupant; such a thing would be a sin against charity or at least against gratitude. Every young maiden is, when dead, a model of purity and candour; every wife and mother an example of fidelity and maternal love ; every soldier, an illustrious defender of his country; every child, a hope cut off; every usurer, a christian at whose door the unfortunate never knocked in vain. Nowhere are the dead more lucky than at Lima. In fact, not only the tombstones of a great number record the virtues which the sculptor is pleased to ascribe to them, but we have also the *Comercio* which publishes for three or four weeks obituary notices written with the fervour inspired by friendship or by the editor's anxious desire to display his elegant and easy style. No one dies at Lima without the consolation of having a necrologist, unless he belongs to a very humble rank of life : however, we have seen the door-porter of a college write an obituary in verse on his unfortunate wife from whom he had been separated for more than twelve years on account of incompatibility of ideas and temper.

A COMUNICADO (1).

A *comunicado* is, or rather was, not long since, at Lima a cause of alarm and terror for the person against whom it was directed; but this perfidious and offensive arm has been and still is so much abused that it has lost its edge, and no longer has much effect either for good or evil.

The most terrible menace that could be made against a procrastinating debtor, a public functionary, or, indeed, any one from

(1) See the preceding page.

whom something was expected or claimed, was to say: *I will put you in the* Comercio; *I will expose you in the public papers; I will give you a lashing in the press; I will reveal your conduct to the public*, etc. By means of a *comunicado,* the boldest man could be brought to terms, because, fearing for his reputation on the one hand, he was, on the other, compelled to defend himself, which is always an unpleasant necessity. The old formula of a *comunicado* was: " Mr. Editor, have the kindness to insert in the columns of your illustrious journal the following fact: *Mr. So-and-so has committed such or such an act; he is a rogue, a thief,* etc."

Mr. So-and-so would commence his reply by saying: " In your illustrious journal of the..., and under the head of..., Mr. N. N., who is no better than he should be, has assailed me with insults; those who know us both are well aware who is in the right; meanwhile, if I have taken the trouble to reply, it is out of respect for the illustrious public, and not to please my libeller, whom I profoundly despise, etc."

These *comunicados,* which at one time caused great annoyance and made many a man pass sleepless nights, now attract little notice and neither destroy nor make reputations.

Some victims of the *comunicado* have adopted a brief system of defence, which has the advantage of cutting short the discussion at its very outset. They request the illustrious public to suspend its judgment on the facts imputed to them. Years and years elapse and the judgment of the public is thus suspended *usque in æternum,* and the whole affair forgotten.

As the most violent and offensive *comunicado* may be addressed to a journal by any person who engages to be responsible for its publication, the *comunicadista* often throws the stone by the hand of another; then, if the individual insulted accuses him, he begs the editors to say that he was not the person who made or guaranteed the assertion in question. The editors can truly assert that the gentleman accused neither sent nor guaranteed the fact; society is then bound to rest satisfied that he who *wrote* the communication is not its *author.*

THEATRE.

We have little to say on the only theatre which exists in Lima. The first dramatic performances in the capital of Peru took place about two centuries since. The most famous were those given in the parvise of the Cathedral.

The first coliseum was erected in 1601, and its profits were destined for the hospital of San Andrés. The theatre was often changed from one locality to another, till that now existing was built, in 1614, at an expense of 62,132 piastres.

In 1852 the Government, as already stated, gave the Beneficencia other property in exchange for the theatre.

The building, both internally and externally, is unworthy of the capital of a prosperous State, and though for years past a project of erecting a new theatre has been under consideration, there seems little probability of early execution.

The performances at the theatre are comedies and operas, with occasional exhibitions of conjuring and juggling.

The circuit of the pit is forty-six varas and a half, and its depth, from the foot-lights to the entrance, seventeen varas and a half. It will seat six hundred and seventy persons.

The boxes, of which there are three tiers, will accommodate six hundred more. There are also a gallery and some corner boxes, so that the theatre will hold in all about fifteen hundred spectators.

COCK-FIGHTING.

Such was formerly the rage for cock-fighting at Lima, that every day, and almost at any hour, groups of people might be seen in the streets standing in rings round couples of fighting cocks. The authorities were at last compelled to put an end to the disorder and disturbance caused by the quarrels of the artisans and servants, who neglected their occupations to attend these cock-fights, and the means adopted was the opening of a circus for this kind of amusement.

Cock-fighting has been prohibited several times on account of the disgraceful scenes and breaches of the peace which occurred in spite of the presence of the agents of authority who presided at the circus; but it has been authorized just as often as suppressed, and there are now cock-fights every afternoon.

The more important fights, on which heavy bets frequently depend are announced to the public by posting-bills, and in the lifetime of Don Alejo, the celebrated *chirimiista* (player on the *chirimia*, a kind of hautboy), who unfortunately has lately died without leaving

Announcing cock-fights.

a successor to play his sonorous instrument, the streets were paraded by an orchestra composed of the said Don Alejo, another negro beating a drum, and a boy carrying, on his head, a cage with a fine game cock in it.

The persons who take an interest in cock-fights are generally of the lowest order, but there are a few amateurs of the more respectable class, and some of even the highest rank.

BULL-FIGHTS.

The Spaniards, says one of their poets, only want *pan y toros* (bread and bulls), and still more bulls than bread. It is therefore not at all surprising that a people of Spanish origin should have an extraordinary predilection for the barbarous amusement of witnessing bull-fights. At Lima, this taste has been quite a passion, affecting all ranks from the viceroy to the very beggar in the streets.

Bull-fights were one of the first amusements introduced by the conquerors, and were made the occasion of extravagant display. The first fights took place in the *Plaza Mayor*. No memorable event could ever happen at that period without being celebrated by bull-fights more or less magnificent, both with regard to the display made by the spectators and to the richness of the *enjalmas* (1) and other trappings with which the bulls were decorated, and the profusion with which the wealthy threw money to reward the address and daring of the *toreros*.

After the erection of the *Circo del Acho* (2) bull-fights were forbidden on the *Plaza Mayor*. The eagerness of the public to obtain seats was so intense that on Sundays, when the fights were to take place, the circus was filled at an early hour in the morning. The ecclesiastical dignitaries, finding that these exhibitions caused the Limanian catholics to forget the first command of Holy Mother Church, made an appeal to the civil authorities and induced them to have the bull-fights on Mondays, so that the people might not be kept from church on Sundays.

Por la mañana á la misa,
Y por la tarde al sermon ;
Y á rezar las letánias,
Al toque de la oracion (3).

The people thenceforth attended the religious services of the

(1) The *enjalma* was a kind of housing either velvet or satin, embroidered and fringed with gold or silver, to cover the back of the bull.

(2) See page 72.

(3) Mass in the morning; sermon in the afternoon; and prayers when the evening bell rings.

Snnday, but they lost their day's work on Monday, when even the
viceroy gave himself a holiday. The judges in the law- courts terminated their sittings at one o'clock, and at the same hour the doors
of the colleges and schools were thrown open. Who would believe
that the priests and monks themselves (notwithstanding the papal
excommunications) found their way to the *Acho*, and witnessed,
with more or less secresy, the proceedings in the bull-ring?

The fights are announced to the public by posters, then by
handbills called *listas,* which are sold about the streets by boys
who cry as they go along : " *Y... á... cularitaá!* (Vamos con las

listas! Here's is the bill of the performance!) ¿ *Quien quiere ver el
primer toro que rompe la tarde?* (Who wants to see the first bull
that will fight this afternoon?)" The last announcement, that which
most excites the enthusiasm of the populace and decides all waverers,
is the procession of the *figuras* and *enjalmas.* The former are large
dolls in paper dresses, which are placed in the middle of the arena,
and are the first objects of the bull's fury. These figures are so con-
trived as to respond to the bull's attack by a discharge of crackers.
The latter are a kind of housing, generally satin, embroidered and
fringed with gold or silver. The sight of the *enjalmas,* the sound of
the drum and the accompaying *chirimia* (1) excite the delight of
the Limanians to the last degree.

(1) Engraving and note, p. 72.

No description could give an adequate idea of the shouting and uproar in the circus of the Acho during a bull-fight. With the loud conversations of the spectators are blended the cries of numberless dealers : ice-men, pastry-cooks, fruiterers, sellers of water, brandy, sausages, ham, flowers, etc., who hurry up and down the seats, offering their wares simultaneously and screaming as loud as they can.

The performance always begins at two o'clock. Before a bull is let loose, and with the permission of the municipal *alcalde,* who presides on the occasion, all the *toreadores* parade round the arena after first saluting the authorities.

At the same moment occurs the *despejo,* which consists in brilliant military evolutions, executed by a corps of troops (1) : then the fight begins. The alcalde has a trumpet through which he speaks his orders, and the door of the *toril* is not opened till he shouts : ¡ *Salga el toro* (let out the bull) !

The principal feats of a bull-fight are : the *capeo* on horseback, which is only in use at Lima. In this attack the dexterity of the rider and the docility of the horse are displayed in a high degree. Though the majority of the *toreadores* have always been Spaniards, the *capeo á caballo* has never been executed by any but negroes and *zambos,* natives of the country. The most highly prized and most valuable horses have been seen to take part in the fights at the Acho, confided to the unequalled experience and agility of the first *capeador* of our day, a negro named Estevan Arredondo.

The *capeo á caballo* is performed in the following manner : the *capeador* takes his stand opposite the door from which the bull will issue, rendered furious by the narrow prison in which he has been confined for some short time previously and further irritated by the goad at the moment of release. Thus posted, the *capeador,* as soon as the bull appears, holds out the *capa* (cloak) and draws him towards the middle of the arena. When the bull's horns are about

---

(1) The engraving at page 72 represents the Plaza de Acho at the moment of the parade executed by a corps of cavalry.

Estevan Arredondo.

to touch the flanks of the horse, the rider promptly wheels round his steed to the right or left, and the bull wastes his strength on the vacant air.

A bull must be very strong to bear, without fatigue, six bouts of the *capeo á caballo.*

Negro *capeador* on foot.

The other feats, called *cupeo á pié* (on foot), *banderillas,* and *espada* (sword), are known in Spain; but the Spanish *toreros* do not surpass the negroes of Lima in these dangerous assaults.

Another feat, quite peculiar to Peru, is the *mojarras.* Several Indians called *mojarreros,* armed with a kind of lance, throw themselves on the ground, there to await the bull, and when he rushes on the group the Indians attempt to spear him wherever they can. The bull returns several times to the charge and treads the unfortunate *mojarreros* underfoot. Some times the animal takes one of them on its horns and plays with the poor fellow as a child might with a shuttle-cock: but the Indian does not give in, and, unless grievously wounded, always has his revenge.

The *mojarrero* never enters the arena till the bull appears to him no larger than a dog. This optical phenomenon is produced in the *mojarrero,* not by means of concave glasses, but by drinking spirits. As soon as the fight begins, the Indians set to drinking: they ask each other at intervals how big the bull looks, and those whose sight is not yet deranged in the necessary degree reply: *"Todavia está grande; ¡ echa otra copa! —* It is too big yet; let us take another glass!"

What has always been, and still is, reckoned the best bull-fight? You must not suppose that the preference is given to one in which the *toreros* have evinced most address and the bulls most courage: amateurs require greater and stronger emotions.

If several horses are dragged out of the circus dead, or at least severely injured; if there are a few *toreros* half disembowelled; if the Indian *mojarreros* have been tossed up into the air; in short, if there have been plenty of wounds and bloodshed, the day is considered brilliant, and if any one has been killed, the crowd will shout: *"Completa! soberbia!* (Excellent! superb!)"

When a bull is killed, the carcass is dragged from the arena attached by the neck to a *carretilla* (a pair of low wheels) drawn by four horses.

---

(1) Darts with streamers, which are thrown at the bull and stick in his skin.

This is the proper place to mention a singular personage whose passion for bull-fights was almost a frenzy, and whose extraordinary address might be reasonably doubted by our readers if it had not been often witnessed by all the inhabitants of Lima.

This individual lived under the protection of a negro whose functions at the circus *del Acho* were merely to put the neck of the dead bull in the collar which fastened it to the *carretilla*. The negro's *protégé* was always in attendance, and as soon as the dead bull was attached to the carretilla, he ran by its side with a speed equal to that of the horses. The door-way, through which the wheels were to pass, was so narrow that when the carretilla approached in a slanting direction our amateur could not run along-side without danger of being crushed against the wall.

At this critical moment when all the spectators, by a simultaneous cry, expressed their fears for their favourite's safety, the object of their solicitude would leap, with all the agility of a ropedancer, on the bull's carcass, and, cleverly maintaining his equilibrium, disappear from the arena amid the enthusiastic cheering of the crowd.

Some four or five years since, the negro died, leaving his dependant to the care of Providence. The humble occupation of the former had not allowed him to save money to provide for his heir. The whole body of *toreros* expressed a wish to take charge of the orphan: but he paid no attention to their offer, and determined to take his chance in the world without any other guide than his own caprice.

His idle habits, neglected education, and ignorance of any trade, made him a vagabond, but one of the happiest that ever existed. Always lodged in the best hotels of Lima, and petted by the inhabitants as well as by strangers, he passed his time lying on the best of sofas. He never staid more than a month at the same house. Contrary to their usual habits, the hotel-keepers supplied him with all he wanted and never presented their bill: to be sure, if they had done so, it would have been useless. For he never possessed any money or thought of payment. His passion for bull-fights continued through life as strong as ever. On the days when they occurred (Sundays now) he was always at the Acho by two o'clock; he accompanied the negro who had succeeded his master, and attended the exit of all the bulls to the last.

His friendly intercourse with persons of fashion, and the confidence they placed in him, gave him such a relish for every kind of feast, that he was a constant attendant on all the public promenades. If he learned that there would be a crowd at Callao or at Chorrillos on the occasion of some public rejoicing, he would take his place in a first-class carriage on the railway, of course without paying. More than once he has been seen seated by the side of the President of the Republic in the state carriage.

He was never known to speak even to the persons with whom he was most intimate. He never read a journal, poster, handbill, or any other announcement of public festivals or rejoicings, and yet he well knew the days for bull-fights, as well as the locality where any amusements were passing. But on no occasion did he ever visit the theatre.

A Spanish torero took him one day to Callao, put him into a boat and carried him on board a steamer by which the Spaniard was going back to Spain. Our hero had never before been on board ship, and yet the excursion seemed anything but disagreeable to him; but as soon as the vessel began to move, he perceived how he had been tricked. Without the least hesitation, he jumped overboard and swam to the pier, where he was received by some mariners who had known him at the Callao circus. From that time forth he would never go on board any vessel. An Englishman having attempted to kidnap him, he fell into a passion for the first time in his life, and, to recover his threatened liberty, gave his abductor a severe bite in the arm.

This lucky mortal, who happily passed a life exempt from all care, paid the debt of nature two years since (in 1864). He died, but his memory will long survive; Lima, or at least the present generation, will not forget the *perrito negro del Acho* (the little black dog of the Acho).

Bull dragged off with the *carretilla*.

When the bull-fights used to take place on Mondays, the promenade of the Acho was crowded on the previous evening; the *Alameda*
swarmed with people going to see the circus watered, an operation
performed by negroes with watering-pots. The next morning, great
numbers also assembled to witness the arrival of the bulls.

The persons who did not choose to enter the circus usually
passed the afternoon in the *Alameda*. Nothing could well be more
diverting than the aspect of this promenade animated by the presence of hundreds of *tapadas* (1), lavishing their graceful wit in the
shrewd repartees for which the Limanian ladies are so famous.
Protected by the veil, which effectually conceals them from all re-
cognition, they gave free scope to their talent and genius, and many
a dandy with great pretensions to wit has been obliged to abandon
the field ashamed at the failure of his batteries. Nevertheless, with
all this liberty of language, the *tapada* never forgot the good-
breeding and dignity of her class : woe to the unfortunate or
blundering wight who attempted to carry matters beyond the limit
traced by the laws of polite usage!

The promenade on the *Alameda del Acho* has not the same attractions now as it had ten or twelve years ago.

(1) Ladies veiled with the *manto*. See engravings, pages 105, 106, and 107.

The passion for attending bull-fights was formerly so overpowering in the inhabitants of Lima, that people thought themselves most unhappy if they could not procure, even at a great sacrifice, the pleasure of seeing a bull die by the hand of a man or a man by the horns of a bull.

To attain this end, many a working man with a large family, if he wished to preserve peace in his household, had to make all sorts of sacrifices in order to procure for his better half the sight of this cruel amusement. Gay women would pawn a jewel or a garment, and, what is scarcely credible, not a few of this class would even pledge their bed to raise money to attend a bull-fight. The rabble, quite as eager for the amusement, and less scrupulous, would procure the necessary means by theft.

In the galleries which surround the circus are stands occupied

Chichera (chicha-seller) of the Acho.

by retailers of brandy and *chicha* (a kind of beer); the crowd can therefore moisten their pleasures or drown their cares with intoxi-

cating liquors; the excitement caused by repeated libations nearly
always leads to quarrelling, sometimes to blows, and fatal conflicts
are by no means uncommon on bull-fight days.

The public authorities, ever *zealous and vigilant*, decreed that
spirits should not be cried or sold within the walls of the *Acho*.
Only the first part of this police regulation has been executed.
Brandy is indeed no longer cried for sale; the dealers now offer
their liquors as *agua de nieve* (snow water), *cebada con piña* (barley
and pine-apple), *las suertes* (the passes).

As to the sale, the authorities have thought proper to make a concession to the dealers, who still vend the same spirits disguised under
the names above given.

NOCHES BUENAS (HAPPY NIGHTS).

Just as in Spain the word *rabon* (long-tailed) is applied to an
animal which has lost that appendage, so in Lima they call *noches
buenas* those nights which in any other country would be rightly
considered as intolerable.

Twice in the year, on Holy Saturday and Christmas-eve, the
principal square is decorated, or, to speak more correctly, made to
assume the aspect of a village-green on a feast day, by erecting
along its four sides a number of stalls or booths, ornamented with
branches of willow, paper flags, and small Venetian lanterns. In
the midst of this verdure and glare, may be seen hanging fowls,
viands of all kinds, especially hams, sausages, etc. The stalls are
covered with children's toys, porcelain, flowers, and cakes. The air
rings with a thousand voices crying *tamales* (maize-flour cakes) and
bizcoches (biscuits), in tones more or less discordant. The deafening
noise of drums, whistles, and *matracas* (wooden clappers), summons
the young generation to the scene where their parents' hard-earned
coins are to be expended. Between ten and eleven the square begins
to fill with people; persons of all classes and conditions hurry to the
spot — monks, soldiers, magistrates, the rich, the poor — in short
every body in Lima visits the Plaza Mayor during the *happy night*

Imp. Lemercier & C.ie rue de Seine 57. Paris

to enjoy the harmony produced by the piercing cries of the dealers, to hear the foul language of the populace half-drunk with *pisco* (brandy), and to inhale the perfumes of burning reeds and highly seasoned sausages.

It is scarcely necessary to remark that every body feels bound to carry home something purchased there; that the youthful lover on that night pays any price that may be asked for a flower as a present to the idol of his heart; that the grave papa expends two *bolivianos* in buying a toy for his son, though the same might be had at any other place and time for one quarter of the sum; and lastly, that the obliging husband pays, without any audible murmur, for whatever his dear wife may desire, though inwardly cursing the high prices of the *happy night.* After midnight, families generally return to sup at home, eating either what they have purchased during their walk or what has been prepared by their own servants. It seems to be a general rule that all the dishes eaten on these occasions should be fat, heavy, and indigestible. Some stomachs however cannot support such food, and an attack of indigestion more or less dangerous is often the consequence. Thus, to walk about for two or three hours in the middle of the night, to have one's ears pierced with yells, and one's nose grievously offended; to have bought articles for many times their value, and lastly to have laid the foundation, perhaps, for a serious illness, is what people at Lima call passing a *happy night.*

AMANCAES. — NATIONAL DANCES.

On St. John's day, the 24th of June, the Limanians begin their excursions to the *lomas* (hills) of *Amancaes,* about half a league from the Plaza Mayor. The landscape is beautiful : the high hills encircling an extensive *pampa* (plain) are covered with magnificent verdure relieved with great numbers of large yellow flowers called *amancaes,* and an immense diversity of flowerets, among which the most remarkable is the *San Juan,* or St. John's flower, so called because it generally opens about that day. Scattered over the plain are numerous *ranchos* (farm-houses) where refreshments are sold. On Sundays and Mondays, when people assemble in greatest numbers, there are harpers and guitar-players at these ranchos, and balls are generally improvised, in which polkas and mazurkas are unknown, and the *zamacueca* is the prevalent dance.

The *zamacueca* was once the most popular national dance; now that the gallop, the polka, and the whirling waltz have exiled from aristocratic abodes the minuet, the *londú*, and the *cachucha*, the favourite dances of our forefathers, the *zamacueca* has also been well-nigh excluded from family parties; nevertheless it still maintains its ground among the working classes, among gay women, and under the ranchos of the *Amancaes*.

As we have thus been incidentally led to speak of our dances, we may be permitted here to say a few words about the masters of the choregraphic art who have gained some celebrity at Lima.

In the Peruvian capital the profession of dancing-master used to be followed by none but negroes and *zambos*. They were classed in several categories. Some, in giving their lessons, used no other music than the voice; others carried a guitar with them; while the first-class masters used the guitars of their pupils. The first category, as a general rule, gave lessons to none but persons of their own class and colour, among whom figured the most popular dancing women (many of them under the protection of the *señors oidores* or judges of the *Audiencia*), who used to attend the famous mulatto balls. Among these masters, the most noted was a negro called Tragaluz (bull's eye), but whether this was merely a nickname or not, we are unable to say. He had the talent of imitating with his voice all the instruments of an orchestra, from the trombone to the flute. Tragaluz adopted a technology of his own for the steps he taught, such as *Figura reale, Tras-piés circonflejo, Paso de sirenita, Cohete de soga falso*, etc.

He also composed music for dancing, and his choregraphic works comprise the *Londú floreado*, the *Valse de aguas*, and the *Cachucha intencional*.

Among the masters of the second category, we must not forget

Elejalde and Monteblanco, both negroes and of the deepest black. Elejalde was distinguished for the waltz and the *zamacueca*. Monteblanco was a man of extremely refined manners; he rose to be the favourite professor of the *señoritas* of Lima, and was even engaged by several colleges. Wishing to give his language all the elegance which he considered obligatory on a professor having to deal with the highest classes of society, he affected a peculiar phraseology. For instance, in saluting one of his lady pupils, he would say : « *Señorita, ¿ como ha sufrido V. el curso de anoche á acá?* (Miss, how has time passed with you from yesterday till now?) » To an inquiry about his own health, he would reply : « *Combatiendo el tiempo y sus estragos, no he sentido detrimento, muchas gracias.* (In resisting time and its ravages, I have experienced no detriment, many thanks!) »

Maestro Martinez belonged to a still higher class. He did not, like Elejalde and Monteblanco, carry with him an enormous guitar decked with ribbons of all colours. Martinez was a negro, of rather handsome person, elegant in his manners, and always well-dressed. His pupils were the daughters of the highest families.

We should be embarrassed to determine to what category belonged the celebrated Maestro Hueso, who died only a few years since. Possibly he possessed nimble legs and feet when he embraced the profession of dancing-master, but when we knew him, though still giving lessons, he was gouty and so crippled with rheumatism, that instead of dancing he could hardly walk. Hueso was a *zambo*, as tall as a grenadier. He always wore a black frock-coat, long and ample, yellow slippers, and a white cotton cap, over which he clapped a broad-brimmed hat. He used to visit his pupils on horseback, and might easily have been taken for a *cirujano romancista* (country doctor), had there not been apparent under his cloak, which he wore winter and summer, the end of the green bag holding the violin from which this choregraphic Mathusalem could extract very melodious sounds when giving his lessons.

All these celebrities are now nearly forgotten. The polka and the waltz would seem to require no masters. The only professor of *piruetas* now in Lima is the Maestro Navarro, a *zambo,* who was originally a saddler, but he seems to have made the discovery that the frock-coat became him better than the leather apron, and that making pirouettes was a far more agreeable profession than handling the awl.

After this slight digression, let us return to *Amancaes.*

On certain days this promenade attracts a great concourse of people, comprising all classes of society. The excursion may be made on foot, in a carriage, or on horseback. Since the introduction of hackney-coaches, the *balancin,* a clumsy kind of vehicle drawn by two horses with a negro as a postilion, has disappeared from the scene. The *balancins* were equally used for airings in town and for

The old *balancin.*

journeys to Callao and Chorrillos. They were invariably drawn by horses as lean as hurdles; so that it became proverbial to say of a man or an animal : *es tan flaco como un caballo balancinero* (as lean as a *balancin* horse). The *balincinero* (driver of a *balancin*) required to be a merry fellow and to know a good number of songs. In fact he never urged on his horses with the vulgar oaths familiar to the drivers of Spanish stages, but only with lively songs.

The *señoras* and *caballeros* of good society ride on horseback in the European style; but the women of the lower orders sit astride like men, in spite of their gowns and petticoats. When a family

Zamba going to *Amancaes*.

has only one horse at command, the husband mounts behind and gallops with his wife.

The exclusive dance at *Amancaes* is, as already stated, the *zama-*

Negroes returning from *Amancaes*.

cueca. The orchestra is composed of a harp and a guitar. To these instruments is added a kind of drum, usually made of a wooden box, the boards of which are partially unnailed to render it more sonorous. It is played by striking on the parchment with the hands or with two sticks. The skill and good ear with which the negro beats the drum, keeps time, and animates the dancers, are really astonishing. As the *cajon* (big drum) is the soul of the orchestra, the *zamacueca* is commonly called the *polka de cajon*.

Negroes dancing the *Zamacueca*.

The music is always accompanied by the voices of two or three negroes; and, at the end of each couplet, the dancers who can or will sing repeat the burthen in chorus. These *finales* are called *fugas* (fugues), and during their repetition, the movements of the dancers become faster and wilder.

The *zamacueca*, though still retaining its choregraphic and musical character, has undergone certain modifications and received different names, having been successively called the *maisito*, the *ecuador*, etc., and at present the *zanguaraña*.

The poets who write songs for the *zamacueca* are not of a very high order. The majority are the *guitarristas* themselves, whose only inspiration is brandy.

CHORRILLOS.

In the months from December to March, which are the hot season at Lima, the wealthier inhabitants of the capital migrate to Chorrillos to enjoy the freshness of the sea breezes. Those whom fortune has not favoured keep as cool as they can in the city : for such is the destiny of the poor, who, in every country have equally to endure the extremes of heat and cold.

The empire of fashion must be indeed despotic to have made Chorrillos the resort of aristocracy and beauty. In spite of the new and sumptuous houses now seen there, the aspect of the place is unpleasing and even repulsive. The streets are narrow and crooked, and, owing to the absence of pavement, it is impossible to take a walk or ride without having one's clothes covered with dust and sand.

What, then, is the attraction of Chorrillos? Why should it be the favourite residence of the aristocracy? Why should a man be considered nobody if he does not spend at least his Sundays at Chorrillos? Why is it the rendezvous of all the loungers of the capital? Is the charm to be found in the temperature or in the sea? Nothing of the kind; but solely in the fact that the goddess Fortune has there established her temples; that the majority of the houses are so many battle-fields in which a constant struggle is maintained, day and night, between the worshippers of Mammon. At Chorrillos a fortune may be won in a day or two, or the savings of a year, nay of a whole life, may be lost in a single night.

Chorrillos is indebted to General Castilla for its most important improvement — the terrace above the *Barranco* (ravine), which commands a charming view of the sea. During the fine summer evenings, when the moon is shining in all her splendour, the numerous but yet select company which assembles there, and the military band, make that walk a truly delightful spot.

View of the quay of Chorrillos.

Before this terrace existed, the life of the ladies at Chorrillos was extremely dull and monotonous. During the evenings especially, they were condemned to solitude, while their lords and masters were revelling in the enjoyment of the *innocent* pastime offered by the gaming-table.

View of General Pezet's *rancho* (country-house).

The houses at Chorrillos retain the name of *ranchos* (lodges), a word originally applied to the habitations of the Indians, who used to let them as lodgings to families of Lima, during the summer season, reserving only just sufficient room for themselves. The In-

Interior view of the garden.

dians have already sold many of their *ranchos,* and on the sites handsome houses have been erected, which will bear comparison with those of the capital. The *little palace* of Señora Elguera is de-

Pescadora of Chorrillos.

serving of especial mention, as also General Pezet's house, which has been built and furnished with a splendour apparently without object at such a place as Chorrillos.

The chief occupation of the *Chorrillanos* (Indians of Chorrillos) is fishing. The women carry the fish to Lima for sale, either at the market or in the streets. Before the railway was made from Lima to Chorrillos, the *pescadora* (fisherman's wife) acted as carrier and messenger to all the families of Lima.

Some time elapsed before the *Chorrillanas* (women of Chorrillos) dared to venture on the railway. They were unable to conceive how carriages without horses could whirl along so fast, *unless the devil had a hand in it.*

Even at the present day, the *pescadora* prefers the jog-trot of her mule, although the quiet animal takes three hours to go from Chorrillos to Lima.

CARNIVAL.

Among the ridiculous diversions which barbarism introduced among nations and the progress of civilization has not yet banished from all countries, must be classed the follies of carnival (Shrove-tide).

Should we attempt to give an idea of what were the diversions of Lima only twenty-five years since, any one would suppose us bent on calumniating its inhabitants and representing them as capable of indulging in excesses which, fortunately, have now disappeared.

Some days before the carnival, the police never fail to publish a notice forbidding any one to throw water from balconies on passengers, or to appear in the streets in disguises, under pain of penalties, which are never enforced. The soldiers composing the patrols, and the officers commanding them, are the first to feel the salutary effects of the order they are charged to put in execution. They never pass through a single street without being sprinkled more than once.

At present we see none of those bands which used to parade the streets, with faces hideously blackened and heads made to look like Medusa's or a demon's. The negresses and *zambas* no longer take possession of the kennels to roll in them men of their own class, and to drench with water all well-dressed people who would not pay toll for a free passage. However, it is even yet scarcely possible to walk the streets without being inundated to some extent. The least to be expected is that your clothes will be soiled by a discharge of dirty water as you pass quietly along about your business. You may consider yourself very fortunate if a cold, or some more serious illness, does not send you to your bed to meditate at leisure, in forced repose, on the pleasures of carnival time.

There are several kinds of *refreshments* in vogue during carnival, but the three principal are : the *catarata* (1), the *geringatorio* (2), and the *proyeccion* (3).

The *señoritas* get their servants to place on their balconies such a provision of water as almost literally to convert them into *cataracts*. The maids are not content to sprinkle you with a ewer or jug; they carry up pails quite full, and project the contents with all the force of their muscular arms.

The wild young fellows who seek amusement in the streets carry with them large pewter syringes and bottles full of water; by means of these instruments, which seldom appear in public at any other time, they squirt water into the balconies. Those who shrink from using this portion of the apothecary's arms, parade the streets on foot or on horseback provided with small baskets containing egg-shells filled with scented waters, flour, or small sugar-plums. This last system has the advantage of breaking the windows, and, if the eggs are flung with a vigorous arm, they may occasionally knock

(1) *Catarata*, throwing water, from a window or balcony, on the persons passing in the street.

(2) *Ceringatorio*, squirting water with a syringe.

(3) *Proyeccion*, throwing of eggs or other missiles, as will be explained further on.

Carnival *caturata*.

Carnival *geringatorio*.

out a young lady's eye, or leave her, in the middle of the face, some lasting souvenir of the carnival.

Lanzadores de huevos (egg-throwers).

In due course, these three days of folly come to an end : many dozen bottles of foul and offensive fluid (ironically called *lavender water*) have been emptied; some hundreds of egg-shells broken, many flasks of brandy drunk, and some little blood also shed, as the natural result of the quarrels and frays engendered by disorder and licence. But on Ash-Wednesday every body recovers his or her reason, to remember that the first man was taken from the dust of the earth, that we ourselves also are dust, and to dust must we return. On hearing the church bells, the most inveterate *carnavalistas* quietly proceed to the sacred edifice, and kneel before the priest, who marks a cross on their foreheads with ashes and water. The venerable matron, who has seen some fifty carnivals, would feel certain, if she had not a few ashes on her forehead, that *the devil in person would take up his abode in her heart.*

CARNIVAL COMPADRES (GOSSIPS).

The usage of choosing *compadres* in carnival has disappeared from the upper classes, but still subsists among a certain set of persons as a means of extortion and imposition. On the Thursday of the last week but one before Shrovetide, the women look round among their acquaintance for those whom they think most generous, and each *comadrera* (gossip) selects as many victims as the extent of her connections allows. At the cost of two or three piastres, or less, she prepares a *tabla de compadres*, which is nothing more

Little negress carrying a *regalo de compadrazgo* (carnival present).

than a large salver covered with fruit, flowers, and a few figures of burnt clay made in the country. But the essential emblem of the *compadrazgo* (gossipred) is a *negrito* (little negro), also of clay, containing a paper on which is written a *décima,* properly, a ten-line stanza of octosyllabic verse, though there are seldom more than four or five lines.

The two following specimens will show what divinity inspires the poets who devote their muse to the composition of *décimas de compadres:*

> Mi querido compádrito
> De toda mi estimacion,
> Te mando mi corazon,
> Y tambien este négrito.
>
> Quisiera tener talento
> Como tengo voluntad,
> Para hacerte conocer,
> Con este hermoso négrito,
> Mi cariño, compádrito (1).

In most cases, the arrival of this present produces anything but a pleasant effect on the *compadre*. If he happens to be a man of limited means, his embarrassment is all the greater, for the *tabla* must be returned on the following Thursday. As the object of the *compadrazgo* is well known, and, on the other hand, pride will not allow him to accept the gift without making some return, he of course sends back a gown-piece, or some other article, worth ten or perhaps twenty times more than the present he received from his *comadre.*

It is considered indispensable that the negress who carries the *décima* should be as handsomely dressed as represented in our engraving.

ALL SOULS' DAY.

On the 1st of November, the festival of All Saints, and the eve of All Souls, great numbers of people flock to the Pantheon or General Cemetery.

1)
> My dearly loved gossip,
> Who hast all my esteem,
> I send thee my heart
> And also this little negro.
>
> I would fain have the talent
> As I have the good will
> To make known to thee,
> With this sweet little negro,
> My fondness, dear gossip.

We know not what pleasure can be felt in visiting this gloomy abode of the dead, where people ought to go only to shed a tear or breathe a sigh to the memory of a relation or a friend. But the fact is certain, that sorrow is the feeling least apparent on the countenances of the visitors, and that their minds are occupied with anything rather than the thoughts of eternity. In the cemetery, as in any other public place, the young gallant pays his court to the fair, and the coquet endeavours to engage the attention of admirers, by displaying to the best advantage her personal charms and her elegant toilet.

There is nearly always a ridiculous side even to the most serious and solemn of human affairs. The ludicrous abuses which have crept into many religious acts will often excite a smile. On All

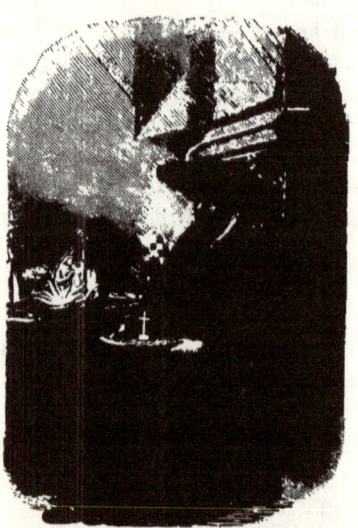

Priest soliciting alms for souls in Purgatory.

Souls'day, the cemetery of Lima is frequented by numbers of priests and young monks *canchadores* who make a trade of reciting the responses for the souls of the dead. They are not ashamed to oppose each other as briskly as the lowest petty dealers. If one offers his prayers for a real, another will take half a real, and some will even throw in three for a real. The Indians of both sexes, who think their relatives' souls may be delivered from purgatory by abundant prayers, are the customers who give most employment to the jaws and tongues of the *canchadores*. According to the proverb : *Como va la paga, va la obra* (literally : as goes the pay, so goes the work), they curtail their prayers to the brief formula : *Ne recorderis peccata mea... Hoo! hoo!... hoo!... in pace, amen.*

During the evening of All Saints and the whole day of All Souls, the bells of every church toll continually for the souls of all the Christian dead throughout the world. We still see at the doors of some churches the hideous display of *calaveras y canillas* (death's heads and cross-bones), for the purpose of stimulating people to give alms, ostensibly for prayers to be said for souls in purgatory, but which undoubtedly also profit some few souls that have not yet left this vale of tears.

PHYSICIANS.

The physicians of Lima resemble those of other countries where there are good ones. The literary and scientific studies determined by the regulations of public instruction, as necessary to confer the right of dispatching souls to the other world, *secundum artem,* and in accordance with the principles of Hippocrates, inspire society with sufficient confidence to place itself in the hands of these *angels of consolation.* A very different state of things existed some eighty years ago. At that period, to be received among the disciples of Galen, all that was necessary was to have the inclination and to be a negro.

If the venerable fathers of medicine could, in the year of grace 1800, have made acquaintance with their brethren in Lima, they would certainly have disavowed their profession, with the regret of having written their gigantic folios to no purpose.

As far back as our memory reaches, we must declare that, with the exception of the respectable physicians named Unanue, Tafur, Heredia, Paredes, and two or three others more or less white, the fairest complexion to be seen among the rest was of the colour of cinnamon. The noble *caballeros* of Lima looked upon the profession of medicine as unworthy of them; the two callings which the master generally reserved for the sons of his slaves, when spoiled by the society of the *señoras*, were those of doctor and footman.

According to the regulations of that period medical men were divided into three distinct categories : 1. the *cirujano romancista* (surgeon who does not know Latin), who could only treat external maladies by ordering topical remedies and plasters, and internally, whey or chicken-broth at the most ; 2. the *cirujano latino* (surgeon knowing Latin) who was permitted to prescribe for more serious cases, to practise serious operations, such as amputations of limbs, and to order purgatives; 3. and lastly, the *medico* (physician proper), who might make use of drugs of all kinds, without restriction, and undertake the treatment of all sorts of diseases.

The *cirujano romancista* was received after a few months' practice at the hospital, and provided he were able to distinguish the cases in which a poultice of marsh-mallows was preferable to one of bread and milk, he was sure to obtain his diploma from the worthy tribunal of the *protomedicato*.

The *cirujano latino* was bound to acquire some degree of skill in the use of the bistoury and the probe, and to have some little knowledge of anatomy.

The *medico* was the *ne plus ultra* of the science. According to the denomination which the Spaniards gave to the men of that profession, the *cirujanos* and *medicos* were called *físicos* (physicians).

Lima still preserves a vivid remembrance of many of its former *cirujanos* and *medicos*. The celebrated surgeon, Roman, will especially pass down to the most distant posterity. By some he was called Doctor *Pescado frito* (fried fish), and by others *el Doctor de las Négritas.* He owed his first appellation to the resemblance of his lean and pointed face to the head of a fish, and the second to his invariable politeness to young negresses. If the *físico* Roman over-

took a cookmaid returning from market with her basket full of provisions, he would pull up his horse to say to her: *Señorita, ayudaré-
mos á llevar la cárga* (allow me to assist you in carrying your basket).
Roman was a *cirujano romancista;* his name and countenance
scarcely permitted him to be anything more, but he was a doctor,
duly graduated, of the Royal and Pontifical University of *St. Marcos*
of Lima.

Nothing could be more curious than the appearance of Doctor
Roman on state days, when there was an official assembly. The
Doctor attended as a member of the illustrious university corps.
Imagine a man almost black, of middle stature, thin, with a head
half covered with grey wool, prominent eyes, hollow cheeks, a
large mouth, and enormous ears; dressed in a green coat, the collar of which rose above the nape of his neck; wearing a cravat of
red silk, the ends of which were passed through a ring ornamented
with an immense stone of the colour of a sapphire; a waistcoat of
embroidered velvet; trowsers of brown cloth, but which he never
allowed to descend below his ankles, in order to show off his silk
stockings; black velvet shoes with silver buckles, a cocked hat
with silk tassels, and the doctor's ermine on his shoulders; silk
gloves with the ends of the thumb and fore-finger cut off for convenience in taking his pinch of snuff; on the index finger, over
the glove, the traditional ring of the *físicos* (that of Doctor Roman
was of brass with a big topaz of the same category as the sapphire
in his cravat), and lastly, a short piece of whalebone for a cane, and
an idea may be formed, although incomplete, of the type, unique
in its kind, of the *Doctor de las Négritas.*

The appearance of the doctor on horseback was not less singular;
he always had horses so lean that the poor beasts seemed as hollow
as violins. One day he thought he had discovered the secret of fat-
tening his favourite animal by giving it gelatine. He administered
that luxury mingled with corn and bran, the whole steeped in water, but the corn and bran were added in such small quantities
that the ungrateful Rossinante preferred to die rather than get fat.
The doctor of former days was easily to be distinguished; a man

The doctor of the olden times.

mounted on a mule or a raw-boned horse; in winter, wrapped in
his mantle, and in summer, screened from the sun under an im-

The doctor of the present day.

Dr. NOHL
Professor at the University

mense parasol; wearing a black hat of cylindrical form, and bearing on his fore-finger a ring generally set with diamonds, was invariably a doctor.

At present, if anything serves to distinguish a doctor from the rest of mortals who ride through the streets on horseback, it is the elegance of his exterior and the beauty of his steed; for, living at a period in which time is money, he no longer travels at a mule's pace but at a horse's gallop.

From the above description, one might imagine that human life in Lima was exclusively abandoned to ignorant and ridiculous charlatans. Happily such was not the case. From the midst of this obscure crowd arose men of talent, who, by their unceasing study, have attained as great eminence as was possible in a country then so distant from Europe. Doctors Valdes, Davila, Faustos, and others besides, were men of colour, but succeeded in gaining a distinguished position as practitioners of great merit. Doctor Montero, generally called *el Doctor Santitos,* a negro as black as jet, was born with a genius for surgery. Nature seemed to have destined him for that profession; for, instead of the huge and horny hands which are generally a mark of men of the negro race, his were small, delicate, and soft as those of a *señorita.* His sight was keen and his hand steady even at the age of sixty. He acquired by means of his constant efforts and long studies such skill in the most delicate and difficult operations that foreign surgeons who have known him were astonished to see him so well acquainted with the progress of surgery and so expert in the use of the most recently invented instruments (1).

THE SOLDIER. — THE RABONA.

In many other countries, the soldier is no doubt better disciplined and more warlike than in Peru, but nowhere is he more obedient,

(1) We have already shown at what period the science of medicine began to acquire a real importance in Peru. See pages 47-49.

patient, and uncomplaining under hardships. The Indian, taken from
his habits of idleness and inertness, endures the hardest fatigues of
the soldier with the most heroic resignation. The Peruvian army,
notwithstanding the laws on recruiting and conscription, and in
spite of the pompous decrees which forbid forced enrolments under
the most severe penalties, repairs its losses and completes its batta-
lions by taking the men it requires wherever they may be found.
In this matter, as in many others, the constitutional guarantees are
purely chimerical, for they do not prevent recruits from being
taken with the lasso like wild animals, marched from village to
village under strong escort, and formed into corps to which the
name of *volunteers* is given, apparently without the least sense of
the inappropriateness of the term.

Indian foot soldiers.

The Indian thus recruited arrives at his regiment, is incorporated
in a company, where he is subjected to all the rigour of discipline

and learns the exercise necessary to make him a worthy defender of the *good cause* and the *national sovereignty*.

An old Spanish proverb says: *la letra con sangre entra* (the lesson must be beaten in with the rod, or literally, the letter enters with the blood). The sergeant's stick is charged with the practical application of this principle. A large number of Indians enter the service without knowing a word of Spanish; they however very soon acquire tolerable proficiency in the use of their arms.

An examination of military corps, commanded by intelligent chiefs who understand their profession, will show that the soldier, in his bearing, whether in the field or at drill, possesses the experience and freedom of movements peculiar to veterans—a fact which proves that the most uncultivated Indian is endowed with great facilities for learning the military art.

Infantry soldiers on the march.

With respect to fatigue, the Peruvian soldier may defy all the soldiers in the universe. He traverses, by forced marches, the most burning sands and the coldest heights, and supports hunger and thirst in an incredible manner. Ten or twelve leagues over rugged and dangerous paths are not too long a march for the Indian, and cause him no weariness. Being excessively sober, a little *coca,*

roasted maize, or a few boiled potatoes arc sufficient food to reno-
vate his strength. After long marches, almost without clothes, and
after suffering all sorts of privations, he fights with courage on the
field of battle, if his chiefs will only set him the example.

The Indian obeys and fights, without knowing whom he is serving
and for whom he is shedding his blood, and without any other idea
than that of fulfilling a duty imposed on him, not by reflection,
sense of duty, or patriotism, but by fear alone; he defends his flag
or abandons it, just as his chiefs follow or betray it.

The Indian is a fatalist, pusillanimous and indolent; he takes
his stand firmly on the field of battle, and will not give way, if no
one else does; he sees his comrades fall around him without feeling
the least emotion, even should they be his nearest relatives; but if
he receives the slightest wound, he will not fire another shot.

The Indian loves the hut which serves as his home, and in which
he lives tranquilly in idleness. If he is torn from it by force, he never forgets his poor cabin, and if any thing should occur to remind
him of his home, he takes advantage of the first opportunity that
arises to return to it. The musical instruments with which the Indian is acquainted and which he plays best are the violin, the tam-
bourine, and a sort of flute which he makes himself out of a large
reed. The flute is well adapted to the melancholy and sentimental
music which characterizes the *yarabi,* or native song of Peru, by
means of which the inhabitant of the mountain expresses his
feelings of love or affliction.

There are few Indians who do not play the flute. When the soldier, far from his hut, hears the tender wailings which issue from
that instrument and remind him of his dear *yarabi,* melancholy
seizes on him and he deserts to return to his cabin. There are officers who do not allow the soldiers to keep this flute, and fear its
sounds more than any other possible cause of desertion.

The necessary adjunct to the Peruvian soldier, and without
which he would have neither resignation nor valour, is the *rabona.*

The *rabona* is the soldier's female companion. She is not always
his legitimate wife, for many of the men leave their spouses in the

village and choose *rabonas*, who become their companions in the field.

In the Peruvian regiments there are no canteen women; indeed, they would be useless, as each soldier possesses a servant who prepares his dinner while on the march, at the camp, or in barracks.

The *Rabona* in barracks.

The *rabona* is also the soldier's washerwoman; she moreover takes care to rid his head of those troublesome guests which infest the woolly hair of the Indian.

The *rabona* is as insensible to fatigue as the soldier; she follows him every where and accompanies him on his marches, however long and painful they may be; her place is with the rear-guard of the corps to which he belongs. The soldier who endures so patiently hardships of all kinds, could not support the absence of his *rabona*.

The officers have sometimes wished to prevent these women from following the troops; but they always found that the men became more irritable, and desertions more numerous.

In the field, the *rabonas* are like clouds of locusts to the districts through which they pass, for they will find food for their soldiers by some means or other. On the march they carry on their shoulders all their kitchen utensils, the little dirty linen they possess, and their child, if they have one, while in their arms they hold a filthy dog for which they have as much affection as for their heroes, if not more.

The *rabona* is much more attached to the flag than to the man; if the latter falls while fighting, she drops but few tears over him, but she sheds them abundantly, if for some cause or other she is forced to quit her battalion.

The *Rabona* on the march.

In return for such marks of affection, the soldier combs his *rabona;* he walks out with her on holidays; he treats her to *chicha* and sometimes to a summary correction. The French proverb, *Qui aime bien, châtie bien* is an axiom for the women of the mountain; as they think, the love of a man for a woman must be measured by the number, frequency, and force of the blows she receives from him. The *rabona* has a lively faith in this principle, carried almost to fanaticism. The soldier and his companion have a weakness for *chicha,* which they often drink to intoxication. It is quite natural then that the Indian should wish to give his helpmate proofs of his tender affection.

The kicks, cuffs, blows with stones, hair-pulling and other caresses of the same kind received by the poor Indian woman, often reduce her to a pitiful state; blood flows from her nose, while her face and head are swelled from the blows showered on her. But woe to

A soldier combing his *rabona.*

any one who, from a feeling of compassion, should attempt to interfere in that love-scene! The Indian woman, who scarcely murmurs under her chastisement, flies into a rage at the officious mediator and apostrophizes him with: *"Mind your business! He has a right to beat me; am I not his wife?"*

In general, the *rabona* belongs to the infantry; as the cavalry corps, being composed almost entirely of negroes and *zambos* from the coast, the women of their villages have neither the strong passions, nor the self-denial and robust vigour peculiar to the women of the mountains.

A *Zambo*, or cavalry soldier.

GUARDIANS OF PUBLIC ORDER.

At the period when lamps in the streets were rare, but thieves were common (1), the safety of life and property depended on the strong arm of the owner.

The terror of the pacific inhabitants of Lima at length reached such a pitch, that the residents of each district resolved to unite to form patrols. Consequently, every evening, ten or twelve men paraded the streets, some armed with pistols others with swords, and many with sticks only. But the persistence of the robbers ultimately tired out the patrols, and numerous complaints addressed to the authorities gave rise to the famous corps of *encapados* (2), charged with pursuing malefactors.

(1) See the article *El Velero* (the candle-seller), pages 205 and following.
(2) So called from *capa*, a sort of cloak.

The *encapados* wore a round hat and a black cape, and carried a coil of rope for pinioning thieves. Before long, the citizens had as much cause to dread the *encapados* as the robbers; for the latter, to assure perfect impunity for their misdeeds, enrolled themselves in the corps of *encapados,* which stratagem procured for them the authorization to carry arms, as well as a disguise.

The *encapados* were subsequently replaced by the *serenos* (watchmen) who werestationed at the corners of the streets, which they were ordered to traverse from time to time. They had also to call out every hour the state of the weather. The *sereno* performed this portion of his duties as watchman by crying out hourly : "¡ *Ave Maria purísima !* (Hail! purest Mary!) ¡ *Las diez han dado!* (Past ten o'clock!) ¡ *Viva el Perú! y sereno (ó lloviendo,* etc.) (Peru for ever! and a fine (or wet) night, etc.)

The *serenos* wore a broad-brimmed hat and short cape, and carried a gun. They were to pass the night without sleeping, but the greater part leaned against the corners of the streets and slept standing. Sometimes, on awaking, they found that a thief had carried off their gun. The *serenos* also had a whistle, which they blew every half hour; this signal had the advantage of serving as a warning to the thieves, who had time to escape when they heard the summons for the *serenos* to assemble.

The corps of *serenos* underwent several reforms. They were afterwards called *vigilantes,* and the people gave to them the name of *corbatones* (big cravats). Later, they were entitled *celadores* (inspectors), and at present they have received the name of *celadores bomberos* (firemen), because they are charged with the service of the fire-engines. The lower classes of the people, seeing that they knew little of fire, except that produced by the consumption of brandy, called them *celadores bombistas,* that is to say, *who pump often*—the bottle. The *celadores* have two uniforms, one for every day and the other for reviews; the latter resembles that of the Paris firemen.

The *celador* of the present day is neither the rascally *encapado,* nor the idle *sereno;* he is a man of a better class, and passes his time seated at the door of a *pulpería* (grocer's shop), reading the

Celador in full dress.

newspapers and discussing politics. An affair must be very serious to excite the attention of the *celador;* nevertheless, although there

Celadores arresting a biscuit-seller.

still remains much to be done, the police-service has considerably improved during the last few years.

The *celadores* are charged with enforcing the strict execution of the police-regulations concerning the cleanliness of the streets, the free circulation in the thoroughfares, and the observance of public decency.

For the pursuit of malefactors outside the city, and in the rural districts, a brigade of mounted police has been organized.

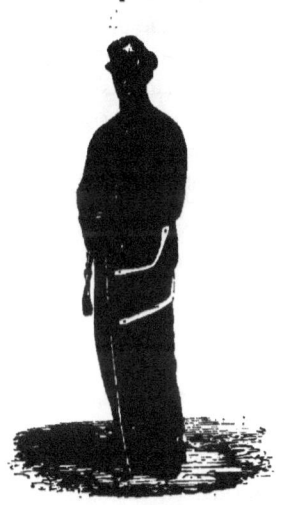

Mounted Policeman.

EL AGUADOR (THE WATER-CARRIER).

Before the creation of the *Empresa de Agua* (Water-works), an enterprise which has proved very profitable to the shareholders, the people of Lima had great difficulty in obtaining a supply of that article under the *despotic monopoly* of the *aguador*. We say *despotic*, and not without reason, for persons who were in want of water could not procure it, if the *aguador* would not supply them. We have also said *monopoly*, because no one could take water at the

12

public fountains to sell, except the registered *aguadores* of each parish.

Servants could only take it for the requirements of their masters, and the poor for their own consumption.

The registering of an *aguador* was an important ceremony. The candidate was bound to present a flask of brandy to his colleagues, and to pay to the alcalde the dues of *media anata* (1), amounting to fourteen reals. The water-carriers of the parish received the new member of their society on the *plazuela* (square), all standing round in a circle, in the midst of which were the alcalde, his clerks, and the probationer. The flask of brandy was passed from hand to hand until not a drop remained. All the company talked and shouted at the same time, which produced a terrible hubbub. The libations being terminated, the newly elected member was instructed in his duties, and then made to swear fidelity and obedience to the alcalde.

The *aguador* of one parish could not take water from the fountains of another.

The *aguadores* were divided into two categories, those on foot and those who were aided by a donkey. The former carried a small barrel on their shoulders; the latter slung two casks across the back of one of those intelligent and patient animals which man so unjustly stigmatizes as the embodiment of stupidity.

It will be readily understood that the *aguador* who possessed a donkey was of a higher class than those who went on foot, either because a larger capital was necessary to set up in business, or because, being perched on his ass, he was in a more elevated position. The *aguador* on foot required only a leather apron, while the mounted *aguador* had to first obtain his donkey, then a pad composed of a number of thicknesses of stout linen covered with pieces of cloth of some bright colour, panniers to hold his pair of water casks, a little bell to announce that his casks were full, a long stick, which he made use of to vault on to his donkey's back, and lastly a

(1) Fine paid on nomination to any office or functions.

cow's rib to tickle the hide of his steed when it did not move along fast enough. The extremities of the stick showed to which category the *aguador* belonged; the ferrule at one end and the forked iron handle at the other represented nothing less than the dictatorial power of the *alcaide*.

Mounted *aguador*.

The *aguador* on foot required, as we have already said, nothing more than a leather apron; the mounted *aguador* wore, and still wears, the same apron, but beneath is a white or coloured shirt more or less artistically ornamented, according to the pecuniary resources of the individual. The *aguador* always carries the scapulary of Our Lady of Carmel, and a leathern purse, in which he formerly kept the ticket showing his exemption from the conscription, and the amount of his day's receipts; at present, the purse contains the money only.

That the ass is an intelligent animal; that by means of training and the stick he sometimes attains the highest degree of knowledge within reach of his species, is a fact proved by examples in all ages and by the writings of numerous historians. From the time of Ba-

laam's ass down to that of Chorrillos(1), history records a series of
donkeys which, if they had only been able to speak, might have
taken part in certain literary or scientific competitions with a fair
chance of success. If the truth of the above were not already demonstrated, the *aguador's* donkey would furnish an eloquent proof.

The *aguador,* who is generally a negro or zambo, may truly be
said to take more care of his ass than of his own children. His donkey
is the object of his most tender solicitude; he would not carry home
a cake for his child, but for his animal he picks up the rind of
water-melons and any other delicacies of the same kind he may
happen to see. This at least proves that the negro is grateful.

The donkey is not only charged with the weight of the water-
casks, to which is added that of his master, but he is an auxiliary
without which the *aguador* cannot rank among the mounted *aguadores;* in fine, he supports the burthen of the entire family, and
may almost be regarded as the *paterfamilias* of the household. The
aguador commences his daily labour by grooming his donkey; he
then gives it a ration of lucerne; afterwards, with the patience of a
good nurse, he spreads on its back several layers of thick cloth to
protect its shoulders; above that he lays one or two pieces of stout
carpet and then the panniers for the water-casks. Some *aguadores*
decorate the head of their animal with ornaments and blinkers of
brilliant colours. Thus harnessed, the donkey receives his master and
then proceeds towards the fountain. The sound of the bell announces, as we have already said, that he has water for sale, although in
the good old times of the monopoly that signal was a complete
mockery. On hearing the bell, the cookmaids, servants, or housewives
cried out to the negro : "*Aguador, echeme U. un viage* (bring me
up a load)," and although, according to the municipal ordinance, the
load, that is, the contents of the two casks, should be charged only a
half real, the *aguador* would reply: "*Está vendio or un rrial vale.* (It
is sold, or, the price is a real.) " Then a dispute arose between the
buyer and seller, but the victory was always obtained by the latter,

(1) See page 107 and following, on religious festivals.

who rode off with his donkey, refusing to sell his merchandise. The *demon of thirst* is a tyrannical one, and will not be trifled with. The *aguador* always imposed his conditions. The persons who occupied the upper stories of the houses were put to much inconvenience and embarrassment from the custom of the *aguador* to reply to them, "*No trepo escaleras* (I do not carry water up stairs)."

In the season when water was scarce, the *aguador*, who perfectly understood the doctrine of political economists "that prices are regulated by the demand and supply," would ask what he pleased for a load of water and always obtained what he demanded.

But as there is no perfect happiness in this rascally world, the sovereign will of the *aguador* was counterbalanced by the still more sovereign will of the parish *alcalde*. The authority of this official was supreme, and his penal code so severe that if the punishments had been inflicted on any other than a negro *aguador*, pity might have been excited for the victim.

The principal modes of punishment were two in number: for a slight irregularity, the *aguador* was temporarily deprived of the right of exercising his calling, but for a serious offence he was condemned to the *enmeladura* (honeying). This penalty was a modifica-

Aguador enmelado.

tion of the *emplumadura* (feathering), which, to the glory of God and Christianity, the Holy Inquisition inflicted on heretics. The

temporary privation, as the expression indicates, was a prohibition
for the culprit to sell water during a certain time. The *enmeladura*
consisted in placing the man on the ground between his panniers
and water-casks, pinioned in such a manner that he could not
move hand or foot; his face and breast were then thickly smeared
with honey to attract the flies, care being taken to expose his face
directly to the rays of the sun.

We must here remark that such punishments were not inflicted
for misdemeanours or cheating to the prejudice of the public, but
for insubordination towards the alcalde or his agents; for quarrelling with fellow *aguadores*, or for selling water out of the parish.

Happily, the penal code of the water-carriers no longer exists; it
is only known by tradition, though the time when it was in force
is not very remote.

Let us now leave the *aguador* and return to his assistant.

Many houses made contracts with their *aguadores;* as soon as the
donkey had been two or three times to a *caseira* (customer's house),
he no longer required to be shown the way; the water-casks being
placed on his back, he would proceed, of his own accord, and at
the precise hour, to serve the customer.

I am not aware whether physiologists or phrenologists have ever
remarked the particular affection of the donkey for the military
art. The asses of the *aguadores* of Lima have given frequent proofs
of this inclination. There still exists (1866) in the parish of San
Marcelo an old *aguador,* whose donkey, the senior of his tribe, obeys
orders with the precision of a soldier.

On arriving at the fountain and the water-casks being placed on
the ground, the negro cries : *Descanso!* (rest!) and the animal lies
down until the barrels are filled. When ready, at the word : *Firmes!*
the donkey is again on its feet. When laden, it obeys the commands
of ¡*Paso regular!* (Steady march); *paso redoblao!* (quick march!)
á la izquier! (to the left!); *frent...!* (front); *alto!* (halt!), etc.

In the parish of the Sagrario or Plaza Mayor, there lived not long
ago an *aguador* named Ño Cendeja, who was well known from
having been successively the slave of a judge and a canon, in which

service he had picked up sufficient Latin to excite the jealousy of a parish priest. ‚Cendeja had also been a soldier; he had preserved his military tastes and above all a great love for the uniform. By a rare coincidence his donkey shared these two predilections. When the animal heard the sounds of military music, he commenced braying lustily. Now let those persons who refuse to admit that donkeys possess any sort of intelligence, furnish an explanation of the following phenomenon.

Rarely a day passes without some military band passing through the streets of Lima. When the music simply accompanied a relief of guards, an escort, or a regiment on the march, Cendeja's donkey confined itself to braying; but if it announced the proclamation of a decree *de buen gobierno* (literally: of good government), nothing could prevent the animal from following the herald through the capital. Neither coaxing, fresh lucerne, nor blows were of any avail. It would break into open revolt against its master, and, by biting and kicking, would force a passage through the crowd till it got close to the soldiers. It followed the music through the streets, stopping each time the decree was read, and when the guard returned to quarters, the animal walked back, humble and obedient, to its ordinary labour. Whence arose this affection for decrees? How could the donkey distinguish what was a government publication from anything else? Cendeja could never solve the difficulty, nor was his sagacious animal able to explain how it came by such knowledge. Another eminent quality in the *aguador's* donkey was its love for its profession; less changeable than man, if the ass abandoned it, the change was never voluntary.

On the road from Lima to Amancaes there is an orchard, the owner of which resided in Lima, and who had in his service an *aguador* named *Laureano*. The public had given to the donkey which carried his water-casks the same name as to the *aguador*. After a few years' residence in Lima, the donkey *Laureano* was taken back to the orchard, but had scarcely arrived when it began to show how deeply it regretted the habits and bustle of town life, and that it had no relish for rural scenes or for the rude simplicity

of its country brethren. It would seem that a long sojourn in capitals, the centres of civilization in civilized States, generally produces a change of feeling, and that neither men nor animals, when
once accustomed to the crowd, can always resign themselves to end
their lives in the solitude, silence, peace, and innocence of the
country. Laureano drooped his long ears; his brayings, like the melancholy strains of Bellini, had no longer, as at Lima, the sonority,

Laureano in the fields.

harmony, and vigour of the creations of Rossini or Mozart; quite
absorbed in his recollections, and borne down by the weight of
overwhelming homesickness, he refused all food and passed his
time in listless apathy.

One day the master ordered Laureano to be sent to carry some
fruit to the market; a pair of panniers filled with apples and pears
were slung across his back, after which he was placed under the
direction of an old negress. Laureano could not support such a hu-

miliation; roaring with vexation and rage, he upset the woman and baskets on the ground, scattering the fruit around him. For six months it was impossible to obtain from Laureano the slightest service for his master. At length one day he was taken to Lima, for some reason or other. He entered the court-yard of the house, but immediately after, without asking permission of any one, he ran off to the *Plaza Mayor*. At the sight of the fountain near which he

Laureano at the fountain.

had passed so many happy hours, he commenced braying, but this time with joy and gladness. He drew near to his former companions and saluted them cordially with friendly bites on the neck; and if the kicks and antics of a donkey could be called dancing, Laureano might be said to have danced with delight. After having given way to numerous demonstrations of pleasure with other donkeys of his age, he returned home again. Laureano was again taken to the fields, but this time he lost patience and went so far as to commit a crime. The animal which had formerly given such proofs of obedience became a *truant*. Baffling the vigilance of his keepers, he stole away, and went at full gallop to the fountain in the square at Lima. It would have been as easy to stay the thunderbolt in its descent, as Laureano in his mad career. On arriving at the fountain he indulged for an hour or two in his joyful liberty and then returned to the house in Lima. The owner, surprised at these daily visits, was informed that Laureano could not get accustomed to a country life, and had him sent back to Lima. But alas! on the day on which he returned to his favourite court-yard, poor *Laureano* probably ate of some poisonous plant or swallowed a spider, for the next day he was found dead, with his venerable head resting on the panniers which he had so long carried on his back. *Requiescat in pace!*

EL CARRETONERO (THE CARRIER).

The negroes who wished to follow the calling of *carretoneros* were subject to the same formalities and to a code not less severe than that of the *aguadores*. As they required a more considerable capital than the *aguador*, they paid as *media anata*, four piastres and four reals, and two flasks of brandy.

The principal business of the *carretoneros* was that of moving household goods in town and country. It was admitted that no article of furniture ever arrived at its destination without suffering some damage. Thence arose a common proverb at Lima: *de que tres mudanzas de domicilio equivalen á un incendio* (three removals are as bad as a fire), because the strongest furniture cannot resist three journeys in a *carreton*.

The corporation of *carretoneros* met once a week to discuss the important affairs of their body. What gave rise to frequent discussions was the tariff for conveyance. Among the number were certain economists so clever that they succeeded in solving the following problem : How the *carretonero* should gain within the year the value of the mule and cart, cover the cost of keeping both driver and animal, and, after paying the daily sum due to his master, have in hand at the end of the year a capital of twenty piastres towards purchasing his own liberty.

Carretonero (carrier).

The majority of the *carretoneros,* like most of the *aguadores,* were slaves who lived away from their masters and disposed of all their time on paying to their owner so much per day. The rate was calculated at one real per day on each hundred piastres the slave had cost. Thus a slave who had cost two hundred piastres paid two reals a day for liberty to work on his own account.

Many *journaleros* (slaves at so much a day) obtained their liberation in a few years and the first desire of a freed negro was to become in his turn the master of other negroes. At Lima, twenty years ago, might be seen a negress cake-seller who had four slaves to carry her baskets.

The heaviest punishment the alcalde of the *carretoneros* inflicted on the members of the corporation was that of the *arco* (bow), which consisted in binding the culprit firmly to one of the wheels of his cart. Some unfortunate negroes have even expired under the torture.

The corporation of *carretoneros,* although composed principally of *bozal* negroes, included among its members some poets of genius, the most remarkable of whom was a little negro named Cayelano, who never spoke in prose.

Negro *carretonero* undergoing the punishment of the *arco*.

For the last thirty years there has been lying in our portfolio, notes of the following dialogue, exchanged between a lady who was about to move and Cayetano.

¿Cuanto quieres por llevar cada carretada?
(How much do you charge for each cartload?)
Para hacé su mecé cuentas cabales.
Pagalá su mecé catorce reales.
(To charge your ladyship a fair price.
I will take fourteen reals.)
¿Quiere V. diez reales?
(Will you take ten reals?)
No, sumecé: lo trato pesa mucho,
Y en ete tiempo la mula está flacucho.
(No, your ladyship, the times are hard
And the mule just now is very thin.)
Vamos, diez reales, está bueno... si no quiere V., veré á otro.
(Come! ten reals; will you take it? If not I will find some one else.)
Mi amita, doce reales, plecio fija.
Así eclíbio el alcarde la talifa.
(My little lady, twelve reals, lowest price.
The alcalde himself has fixed the tariff.)
Pero cuidado con romper nada.
(Take care to break nothing.)

No tiene sumecé cudiao, amita,
Llevalemo depacio la mulita.
(Never fear, my little lady,
I will drive as gently as possible.)

When Cayetano, sitting on the shafts of his cart, passed near a little negress or *zamba* who caught his eye, he would address her in improvised verses somewhat like the follwing:

Ven, zambita de mi vida,
Zamba de mi corazon;
Vamos á dar un paseo
Dentro de mi carreton.

Si conoces, zamba linda,
El amor de un caballero,
Ven, zamba, conocerás
El amor de un carretonero.

Dicen que Dios de los cielos
Murió clavado en su cruz;
Así muere Cayetano
Por la negrita Jesus (1).

EL VELERO (THE CANDLE-SELLER) AND TWO STORIES.

The *velero* hawks about his wares. The article sold by this itinerant dealer is daily losing its importance in consequence of the progress it has itself promoted. We will explain this proposition, which at first sight might be taken for a paradox.

(1)   Come, little zamba of my life,
Zamba of my heart,
Let us take a ride
Together in my cart.

If thou hast known, fair zamba,
The love of a cavalier;
Come, zamba, thou shalt know
The love of a *carretonero*.

They say the God of heaven
Died nailed unto a cross;
So also will Cayetano die
For the little negress Jesus!

Eighty years ago the inhabitants of the *Heroica Ciudad de las Reyes* (heroic City of Kings) only burnt candles of black tallow in the principal apartments of the house, such as the drawing-room and the bed-room; the other portions were lit with rude lamps containing fat or lard, in which was implanted a coarse wick.

A little later (and this was the age of prosperity for the *velero*) the principal apartments were lighted with *velones* (large candles) of white tallow, and the other rooms with *velitas* (small candles) of the same colour. The candles of black tallow were left to the poorer classes, and the rude lamps were no longer seen any where but in kitchens.

This was the age of candles, large, middle-sized, and small (*velones, velitas* and *veloncitos*).

The first period of decay in the manufacture of native candles at Lima commenced with the introduction of wax-lights, which were used in the drawing-rooms, whilst the tallow-candles were relegated to the rooms of minor importance and to kitchens.

Negro *velero* (candle-seller).

Oil lamps, to be suspended from the ceilings, next made their brilliant appearance; we cannot however explain why they were called *reberberos* (reflectors). They naturally occupied the apartments lighted until then with wax-tapers (last period of decay).

This innovation was immediately followed by that of table lamps, and the wax-lights were at once circumscribed to a still more narrow circle (period of fatal crisis for the manufacture of tallow candles).

Gradually the use of oil lamps of all sorts, forms, and dimensions became general in Lima; finally, gas with its dazzling rays was introduced. *Before the brilliant majesty* of its light all others were eclipsed, and the manufacture of tallow-candles fell into mortal convulsions. That branch of industry, which in its time *enlightened* our worthy predecessors, now only exists among a small number of persons who still think with a sigh of the golden age of tallow-candles.

Certain subjects have such an intimate connection between them, that when we speak of one, it is impossible to overlook the others.

How, indeed, is it possible not to retrace the history of public lighting, when we touch even incidentally on the subject of domestic lights?

In the primitive age of Spanish rule, Lima could hardly be said to be a brilliant city, or its inhabitants to live in anything but an age of obscurity. The streets were then plunged in *perfect* darkness; or, as the women said, they were *negras como boca de lobo* (black as a wolf's jaws). Naturally such a state of things was favourable to lovers and thieves; the latter especially profited so much by the darkness that after seven in the evening nothing was heard in the streets of Lima but cries of *ataja! ataja!* (stop! stop!) raised against the *arranchadores* of mantles, hats, and pocket handkerchiefs.

All things have their period of infancy; that of public lighting in Lima consisted, in 1592, in nailing up at the corners of the streets small earthern lamps filled with grease. The air gives life to combustion; but as an abuse of food produces apoplexy, so too much air extinguished the lamps notwithstanding the careful watching of the men to whom the public lighting was entrusted. Experience is the best guide; that it was which taught our ancestors that the

lamp exposed to the wind was as brilliant as a dumb orator is eloquent. The lamp was consequently next placed in a tin lantern. By
means of this precaution, the lamp at length spread for a couple
of hours every evening its wretched light, its thick smoke, and its
delicious perfume, so that the attacks on the wearers of cloaks and
hats no longer commenced before nine o'clock.

Somewhat later, an ordinance declared that the public lighting
was insufficient and of too short duration, and imposed on the citizens, under the penalty of a fine, the obligation of placing at their
doors a lantern which should burn until ten in the evening. This
innovation, which marks the second period of progress, produced
at first an advantage to the tinmen, who manufactured all kinds of
lanterns, from microscopic ones destined for shopkeepers and the
poor, to colossal lanterns with five branches, which first served to
light up the drawing-rooms, and subsequently were suspended at
the outer doors of houses on the occasion of extraordinary illumi-
nations.

Then might be seen, in the same street, lanterns of all sizes containing tallow candles or glasses filled with odoriferous *higuerilla*
(castor oil). The manœuvres of the thieves against hats and mantles
then only commenced at ten o'clock.

Although this measure greatly improved the public lighting, the
ill-will of some, the poverty of others, and especially the initiative
of the Government, gave rise to a system of lighting by means of
lamps placed at the top of stout iron columns or suspended by
chains fixed across the streets. From that moment the public lighting may be said to have fulfilled its object. Thanks to this improvement, with other measures to which we have referred in the article on the *guardians of public order,* an end was put to the robberies
of hats and mantles in the public streets.

This last mode of lighting was at length replaced by gas, which
was used for the first time in the streets of Lima on the evening
of the 7th May 1855.

Such is the history of public and domestic lighting at Lima. It
would have been natural to write that of chandeliers, lanterns, and

lamps; but this has not followed the same course as the other. At the period of insufficient lighting, the houses of the wealthy classes displayed chandeliers and candelabra of great value in solid silver, although the poorer could only procure earthen lamps. At present a person must be in a state of extreme indigence not to possess a brass candlestick or a lamp for burning petroleum. The most wealthy families have lamps and candelabra of exquisite artistic workmanship, and in excellent taste, but... gold and silver only give their colour and brilliancy to the outside of these articles. In this respect, if we have to record the progress of art, we must also notice the decline of the splendour and opulence which not long since still reigned at Lima.

BISCOCHEROS (PIEMEN).

The *biscocheros* are generally Indians or *zambos,* employed by pastry-cooks to hawk their wares about the streets and receiving a certain percentage on the sale. The biscochero, to increase his profits, has introduced the game of the *mósquita* (little fly).

All the dainty articles carried by the *biscochero* on his portable stand not being of the same price, and the young Limanians not having always six, twelve, or twenty *centavos* (half-pennies) at command, the crafty dealer has hit upon an easy means of enabling them to obtain the coveted viands : he sets down his table, which is soon surrounded by an eager group of boys, each of whom stakes two or three centavos at most on the cake or pie he likes best ; the *biscochero* then flicks away the flies with a feather-brush or napkin. They soon return, and the first of the pies selected by the little gamblers on which a fly alights, belongs to the person who staked on it. The others have lost their money; and the biscochero is the only winner if the fly settles on an article on which no one has played.

The *biscocheros* parade the streets at all seasons of the year, from early morning till three or four in the afternoon. Their cries are greatly diversified in words and tone, but during the Holy Week

13

The *biscochero* (pieman).

The *biscochuerela* (pie-woman) of the railway station.

hundreds of them pass along the streets, all shouting : ¡*Pan de dulce!* ¡*pan de dulce!* (sweet cakes!) as loud as they can, in every inflection of voice.

Pastry and cakes are sold not only in the streets, but also at the bake-houses and in different shops.

The most popular piewoman of the present time has her stall at the station of the Lima and Callao railway. Her portrait is given above.

EL PANADERO (THE BAKER).

The *panadero* does not hawk bread, for that necessary is sold only at the bakeries and in shops.

The *panadero* merely delivers bread ordered beforehand. Mounted on a mule, he carries a supply to the retailers and to the houses

Baker delivering bread.

of his regular customers, announcing his arrival by striking his bridle reins against his panniers or leather wallets.

LA LECHERA (MILKWOMAN).

The *lechera* carries milk round to her customers, of course with a due admixture of water.

The *lechera* (milkwoman).

The milkwoman, usually an Indian, brings milk to Lima from the farms in the environs, some at a considerable distance, and makes known her presence by crying : ¡ *La leche-e* ! (Milk-ho!)

HELADEROS (ICE-MEN), TISANERAS (PTISAN-SELLERS), CHAMPU-SERAS (CHAMPUZ-SELLERS), CHICHERAS (CHICHA-SELLERS).

To cool their hot blood was the first care of the old generation; when we say old, we do not go so far back as the days of our grandfathers, because the Limanian appears to have become less heated only about twenty years since, when the class of persons who made a trade of carrying round refreshing beverages to private houses totally disappeared.

There were many sorts of refreshments patronized by the ladies of Lima, for we must observe that the *señoras* seemed to be more addicted to the use of morning refreshments than the *caballeros*.

Then, as now, the *heladores* (ice-men), who are mostly Indians from the other side of the Cordilleras, passed along the streets crying : ¡ *Eh riqui piñi!* (rich pine-apple ices!) *y de leit!* (and ice-creams!) The richness of the ices, if they are pine-apple, consists in containing as little as possible of that fruit; if they are cream, in having merely a dash of milk just to give them a colour. The cleanliness of the iceman is well matched with the quality of his

Indian *heladero* (ice-man).

merchandize; for as soon as his ice-pail is emptied, he washes it very carefully in the street gutter, which receives all sorts of filth from the houses. The *heladero* only sells to the poorer classes, the wealthier having recourse to well-managed establishments which supply ices of excellent quality.

The *tisanera* and the *chichera* held the second rank among dealers in refreshments. The *tisanera* was nearly always a stout old negress, who carried on her head a large basket containing a num-

Negress *tisanera*.

Negress *chichera* (*chicha*-seller).

ber of earthen pipkins, full of a dirty-looking fluid, in which fragments of pine-apple rind might be seen floating.

The *chichera* was likewise an old negress, but of spare figure, and she carried on her head a large earthen jar, full of the precious liquor called *chicha terranova*.

The arcades of the Plaza Mayor used to be occupied by these dealers in ices and cooling beverages. The history of Lima will long preserve the memory of *Ña Aguedita,* whose cooling compounds and *mazamorras* (1) gave her greater celebrity in Lima than the inventor of the electric telegraph enjoyed. *Ña Aguedita* sold refreshing

Fresquera and *champusera.*

beverages in the morning, and in the evening, she also offered her customers *mazamorra morada* and *champuz de agrio y leche* (curds and milk acidulated with lemon). The highest people of Lima would take their seats on the benches of this old matron. Her *chicha de piña* (pine-apple), *chicha de guindas* (cherries), *horchata* (orgeat)

(1) This was a favourite dish in Peru, being composed of Indian meal, honey, and sugar. The *mazamorra morada*, mentioned below, was the same preparation coloured with mulberry or cherry juice.

and *agua de granadas* (pomegranate water), exposed in capacious earthen and glass vases, excited the appetite, or rather the thirst, of the public. Of how many scenes of gallantry have those benches been the silent witnesses! How many happy marriages have been brought about by an invitation to take a cup of *champuz de leche!*

But *Ña Aguedita* was not immortal; she died, and her death marked an epoch of decline in the refreshment trade. In vain did other establishments present, under pretty blue and white awnings, a similar display of vases filled with cooling beverages; they could never obtain the patronage of any but the lower orders. *Ña Aguedita* had neither awnings nor ornaments, and yet there were evenings when it was as difficult to find a seat in her establishment as to obtain tickets for the first performance of a new play by a popular author.

The higher classes no longer take refreshments in the open air, since they have lost their favourite *fresquera.*

At present, there are no *fresquerías* in the Plaza Mayor; the persons who follow that trade have retired to hide its decline in holes and corners.

Public opinion attributed a thousand salutary qualities to these different beverages, but the *chicha terranova* stood first of all. It was regarded by the populace as a sovereign remedy, comparable to nothing but the *elixir of immortality.* Nevertheless the *chicheras* have disappeared: only a single one remains, and unfortunately her four score years and odd leave little hope that she will long remain to dispense *chicha* in this sublunary state of existence.

FRUTEROS (FRUITERERS).

Fruit is sold at Lima in shops, in the markets, and about the streets. The hawkers announce their wares with different cries uttered in a great variety of intonations. The *melonera* rides through the streets on an ass or mule, crying : ¡ *Se va la melonera, la sandillera... la sandillé... la melonié...!* (Here goes the hawker of melons and water-melons!) or else she takes her stand at the corner of

Melon-hawker.

some street and there disposes of her stock. In the former case, she sells only whole melons, in the latter she retails them in slices.

Melon-woman at market.

In the valleys near the capital the *granadilla* (sweet calabash) grows in great abundance and is brought to town for sale by the Indian women, who, instead of crying them along the streets, enter the houses, with the inquiry: *¿No mercas granadillas?* (Won't you buy some granadillas?)

Indian selling granadillas.

The fruiterer who may be called *universal,* because he does not limit his trade to a single article, and is certainly the most popular, as he can suit all tastes and purses — the fruiterer whom the children are most anxious to see, is one who, mounted on an ass, with two large panniers before him, sells the produce of the *huertas* (orchards) of the capital and its environs.

The sale of fruit was formerly monopolized by the *bozal* negroes and negresses, who had a peculiar cry to make known their presence.

These negroes have since been succeeded by the Chinese, who have not half so good a *knack* of crying their goods.

Chinese fruit-seller.

The negroes used to go through the streets, crying: ¡ *Eh frutee!* *pela, pelia!... canasta llena... tamalito de uva! melocotone!* etc. (Here's the fruitman! pears! baskets full! parcels of grapes! and peaches!)

The *canasta llena* and *tamalito de uva* made the children quite wild. The former were small baskets full of ripe apples and pears, and were sold for a half or quarter real; the latter consisted of a good quantity of grapes detached from the stalk and wrapped in plantain leaves. Neither of these articles had a very attractive appearance; but for the *niños*, it was a moment of supreme delight when the *casero* (fruitman) handed them the object of their desires.

MANTEQUERO (LARDMAN).

The *mantequero* does not hawk his goods, but carries them to retail-shops and markets. *Manteca* is hog's lard, which, by certain manipulations, has lost its original taste and smell. At Lima, cooks do not use oil, or butter, or beef fat, but hog's lard, which is certainly superior to the best fat obtained from the ox in Chili.

Negro *mantequero*.

PAST AND PRESENT CELEBRITIES.

Lima has been considered by many persons as the cradle of those whom the Gospel calls *poor in spirit,* and this opinion has so far prevailed that the word *Limeño* (Limanian) has come to be used in Spanish as synonymous with *tonto* and *mentecato* (*silly* and *foolish*).

There was some reason for this opinion, for the education which the nobility gave to their *señoritos* was better calculated to make them idiots or simpletons than men fit to live in this world, where artlessness and innocence are too often the objects of mockery and derision.

It is worthy of remark that, since the extinction of *nobility* and the spread of education, what was called *candidez* (silly simplicity) has ceased to exist in Lima. We feel bound to observe, however, that in speaking as we have done above, we have no intention to disparage or offend persons of noble birth, for our principle, like all others, admits of exceptions.

The son of a nobleman used to pass the first years of his life among *zambas* and mulatresses. When no longer a baby, he nevertheless still remained in the hands of the same class. Instead of playing at soldiers, at peg-top, or kite-flying, his amusement consisted in dressing dolls; and, when grown older, he was allowed to play at the *altarito* (little altar) and say mass. At ten years of age he was unable to read, because *sus señores padres* (his honourable parents) being rich, there was no necessity to puzzle his tender brain. In summer the boy never went into the street, because the sun might tan his delicate skin; in winter he was kept in doors lest he should take cold; when it rained, for fear he should catch the ague; and lastly, if the wind was high, he must not go out because the dust might be blown into his eyes. Being thus always in the society of servants, the youth attained the age of twenty with no other acquirements than being able to talk like the lowest of the populace. He believed in witches, goblins, and ghosts; he durst not enter a dark room, etc.

The populace of Lima, especially the women, and more especially the *zambas* of great families and convents, used a peculiar dialect which has supplied many words to our most noted poet, Don Felipe Pardo, for his keen satires. The *zamba* never said *dedo* (finger), but *dero;* nor *cadena* (chain), but *carena;* in compensation, for *raso* (satin), she said *daso;* for *su merced* (your worship), *sumedced,* etc. The *señoritos* (young noblemen) spoke in precisely the same manner, and remained *señoritos* even after they had become grandfathers. For the nurse-maids, servants, and friends of the family, a Don Juan who had seen sixty summers was always the *niño Juanito* (little Johnny); a Don Manuel, *el señorito Manonguito;* a Don Francisco, *el niño Panchito;* a Don Lorenzo, *el niño Lolito.*

So much for the *señoritos* (boys); as for the *señoritas* (girls), their education was still more neglected. Above all, a woman must not know how to read or write, for fear she should receive love-letters, or, still worse, answer them. To fulfil her mission on earth, the *señorita* must pass her childhood in the society of negresses and dolls, her youth with monks, and the rest of her days, either with the husband chosen by her parents, or serving God, shut up in a nunnery.

There is, then, nothing astonishing, if men, effeminate, ignorant, full of absurd prejudices, without any of the qualities requisite for social life, acquired the epithet of *fools;* but it would be most unjust to infer that *tontería* (imbecility) is the essential characteristic of the Limanian.

Let us pass to another category of *fools,* whom we may call *public buffoons,* since every body has the right to divert himself with them.

In the foremost rank stands one *Don Ñor Bernardito,* who lived about thirty-five years since. His *talent* (for public buffoons must have some *talent*) consisted in imitating *a childbed scene, the noise of fireworks, and the chanting of vespers.* During his performance, *Ñor Bernardito* covered his face with a handkerchief, and imitated the cries of a woman in labour, the voice of the midwife, and the wailing of the new-born child. He next imitated the explosion of rockets, then the music and chanting of vespers.

There was a contemporary of Don Bernardito, but long his survivor, named *Basilio Yeguas,* whose only talent consisted in talking nothing but bad Latin.

Basilio passed his days and evenings at the *Café de Bodegones,* in the street of the same name, where he picked up ends of cigars, as well as the bits of bread and sugar left by the customers of that establishment. The pockets of his trowsers and waistcoat, in addition to his hat, were literally crammed with cigar-ends, bread, and sugar. He used to walk round all the tables, to drink whatever coffee, tea, or chocolate was left in the cups.

The street boys, who, in every city of the world, run after eccentric characters, as if to aggravate their folly, would often hold with Basilio a dialogue something like the following :

" How are you, Basilio?"

" *Bonorum,* hombre (man), *bonorum.*"

"Whence come you?"

" *De Bodegonorum.*"

Dasilio Yeguas.

Manongo Moñon.

" How many cups have you taken?"

" *De cafetorum, cuarentorum* (forty); *de chocolatorum, dieziocho-rum* (eighteen)."

" What have you got in your hat?"

" *Cigarrorum, panorum y azucorum* (cigars, bread, and sugar)."

After the classical Latin of Basilio Yeguas, we must not forget *Benito-Saca-la-pierna,* whose talents consisted in declaiming against the fair sex and in imitating military music.

Benito died some years back, leaving as the only representative of this *talented race,* the least pleasing buffoon that can be imagined.

Manuel Muñoz has no other talent than that of being a knave and of talking so as to be scarcely understood. He calls himself Manongo Moñó, and is consequently generally known as Manongo Moñon. Always intruding into the apartments of the *señoritas,* he has adopted the profession of dealer in cast-off dresses, and may be seen walking the streets laden with female apparel.

The individual of whom we have next to speak, and who died some few years ago, belonged to the Diogenes family, not to the buffoons.

Don Angel Fernando de Quiroz was born of a distinguished family of Arequipa, and received an excellent education.

We know not what causes led this man, who might have occupied a high position in society, to adopt the cynic's mode of life, and to be always filthy and ragged. He was very fond of reading and usually had a quantity of books under his arm, covered by his cloak, which made the boys call after him to ask : *¿ Se vende ese gallo?* (Is that cock for sale?) Quiroz was a poet, and very few nurselings of the muses have written more verses than he. His favourite composition was the sonnet. No important event could happen in any quarter of the world without his making it the subject of his verse.

From Galileo to Newton, from Arago to Don Mateo Paz-Soldan, from Cæsar to Bolivar and Napoleon III, from the wars of Jugurtha to the peace of Villafranca, and from Pius IX. to Garibaldi, all men of note, all remarkable events of ancient or modern history have supplied him with the materials for so many sonnets. Some years before his death, Quiroz was content to write his poetry and recite it in public, even in the street, to all who wanted, or did not want, to hear it; but at a later period, he was seized by such a passion for fame and glory that he published his works under the title of : *Delirios de un Loco* (Ravings of a Madman). He then became as anxious to obtain purchasers as he had formerly been to find hearers.

Don Angel Fernando de Quiroz.

Quiroz was concerned in several family lawsuits, and he possessed a small income. When he received the latter, he immediately employed it in paying the booksellers to whom he was always indebted, the grocer who trusted him for candles, and some other creditors. The rest of the year he lived on small loans obtained from his numerous acquaintances.

The only furniture found in the chamber occupied by Quiroz was a candlestick and a bath, which last served him as a bed, and in which he always slept with his clothes on. One morning this modern Diogenes was found lying motionless in his tub; he had ceased to live.

14

THE SCHOOLMASTER.

A class which has now completely disappeared is that of the old schoolmasters, who have been replaced, we know not with what advantage, by the directors of private *colleges.*

Elementary education was an article to be obtained at Lima, some forty years ago, in two kinds of establishments, the *migas* (1) and the *escuelas* (schools). The former were kept by respectable matrons, some few of whom were negresses and *zambas,* and the name of *migas* was given to them because they admitted children of both sexes. The *escuelas* were managed by *learned professors* and received boys only.

The different steps of instruction were designated by the names of *tablita, cartilla, caton, libro, carta,* and *proceso.*

In the *migas,* pupils advanced to the *carton;* the *tablita* was a small board on which was pasted a printed paper containing the letters of the alphabet in very large type. There was always a cross before the A, and the child who began to use it was said to be at his *cristo* (criss-cross row), or at the *tablita.* The *cartilla* contained a few combinations of syllables, and the *caton* all the prayers in the catechism. The *catones* preferred by the schoolmasters were those which had the picture of St. Cassian on the first page. At the *migas* the pupils also learned the first prayers and chanted them in chorus every afternoon.

The *escuela,* of course, gave more extended instruction. The pupils there studied the *libro* (book), the *carta* (manuscript), and the *proceso,* which last was the crowning feat as regards reading. It seems that, in all countries, lawyers make a point of writing badly, as if a remnant of modesty compelled them to conceal their skill under an illegible scrawl. The *procesos* were scraps of law writings which the *maestros* purchased of the lawyers.

In the schools also instruction was given in writing and in the

(1) The Spanish word is *amigas,* which means seminaries for young ladies.

first four rules of arithmetic. Thus, it was said of a boy whose education was finished, that he could *read, write,* and *cast accounts.*

In the *migas* the charge for a boy or a girl was four reales per month, or perhaps a piastre (4 shillings), if the establishment were of a superior kind. As the *maestra* (mistress) always paid special devotions to some one saint, the children were expected to contribute to her worship by occasional presents.

In the *escuelas,* the *mesada* (monthly pay) varied from one to two piastres, but each of the children had also to give the master, every Saturday, a *rosca de manteca* (round lump of hog's lard). If the unlucky youngster forgot it, or damaged it by the way, he was punished. The masters thus found themselves in possession of forty or fifty lumps of lard, far more than they could consume in a week. They accordingly, in their wisdom, resolved that their pupils should thenceforth bring, instead of the *rosca,* a *propina* (present) of half a real every week.

The *maestro, ayo,* ou *señor* (for he was called indifferently by any one of these titles), was generally a man whose principal *method* consisted in severity.

At the time of which we are writing, knee-breeches had already gone out of fashion, but the respectable corps of pedagogues still retained them. The *maestro* therefore wore breeches, a long black surtout reaching to his ankles, velvet shoes fastened with wide black ribbons or huge silver buckles; a wide fluted frill down his shirt front; a white cravat, and a cotton cap of the same colour. As a sign of his authority he always had in his hands a *ferula* and a whip of several thongs.

The boys, in addition to their school duties, were also accustomed to act as his servants. During the week, they fetched him snuff, cigarettes, sugar, candles, etc. On Saturday, they were obliged to sweep out the school, to clean the benches, to wash the broken bottle used by the master for an inkstand, and burn an old sock to make tinder for him. Saturday was naturally the day which the boys liked best.

The ordinary school punishments were three in number: 1. to remain kneeling for a certain time in the middle of the school-room; 2. the *palmeta* (ferula), which consisted in receiving on the palm of the hand several sharp blows inflicted with a wooden instrument about three inches wide at the end, half an inch thick, pierced with several holes, and terminating in a handle of proportionate length; 3. the whip, which, for any serious offence, was vigorously applied outside the clothes wherever might happen; but in aggravated cases, the boy was horsed and the blows inflicted on a bare part of his person which need not be more particularly designated.

Schoolmaster.

As a general rule, the *señoritos* (sons of gentlemen) went to school accompanied by negro servants, of about their own age. The schoolmaster paid most attention to teaching the *señorito,* and the negro was responsible for his young master's misdeeds or short-comings, which were punished on the poor servitor's person, and his chastisement was considered a sufficient correction for the real delinquent's faults. What a splendid lesson of justice!

The most terrible days for the pupils of a school were those on which the outraged law gave satisfaction to offended society by

hanging a criminal on a gibbet or placing him on a bench to be
shot to death by soldiers. On these solemn occasions the schoolmasters used to conduct all their pupils to the *Plaza Mayor*, the
usual place of execution. After the horrible scene was over, they
returned to the school. The outer door having been closed, the
master, whip in hand, like Jupiter with his thunderbolts, began
lashing about him right and left, declaiming, amidst the cries and
tears of the boys, against vice and crime, and on the sad end which
awaits the guilty. This shower of stripes was called *el juicio* (the
judgment). The day after an execution, the boys would ask each
other : ¿ *Como te fué ayer con el juicio*? (Now did you escape yesterday in the judgment?) After these balmy days, with their lumps of
lard, money presents, and judgments, there came a time when the
career of professor was adopted by men, who, having been unable
to succeed in anything else, thought they possessed just the proper
quantum of ignorance to become schoolmasters. We one day asked
the director of a *colegio de instruccion primaria* why he had placed
the following announcement over his door : *Aqui se educan niños y
niñas de los tres sexos* (House of education for boys and girls of the
three sexes). He replied, with an air of great self-complacency, that
his school was divided into three departments : one for boys, a second for girls, and the third for pupils of either sex. It would have
been most unreasonable not to be satisfied with this explanation.

At Lima there are now neither *migas* nor *escuelas*, there are only
colegios. Any one is free to open an establishment of this kind, if
he will just save appearances by observing certain formalities pre-
scribed by the laws. There are *colegios* for young ladies, in which
the whole number of officials, including the directresses and professors, does not exceed *eight* persons. But, in all these houses, there
are public examinations every year; printed programmes are distributed, and all the principal inhabitants are invited to attend. On
the last day, or rather the last night, of the examination, there is a
grand party, or supper, or ball, and perhaps all three. On the following days, the *Comercio* publishes a report of the solemnity, gives
a glowing account of the great number and respectability of the

attendance, speaks highly of the ready and correct replies of the pupils, extols the skill of the examiners in showing off the talents of the young people; praises the zeal and capacity of the teachers, and, lastly, expatiates on the high moral tone and wisdom of the directors, their devotedness, and affection for their pupils.

¡VAYA UN NUMERITO! (COME, BUY A NUMBER!)

Under the name of *suertes* (lots) a kind of lottery was established many years ago, the profits of which were given to the hospital of San Bartolomé. The price of the tickets was one real, and they were sold by persons whose sole occupation was to go about the streets announcing them for sale by the cry placed at the head of this paragraph. In all classes of society, and among all professions, men of genius are to be found : thus, among the ticket-sellers of former days, there were two famous not only for the popularity they enjoyed and the great number of tickets which they sold in consequence, but also for their power of *ruling fortune*. When a ticket sold by one of these dealers came up a prize, he was said to have *ruled fortune*. These two men were best known by nicknames, one of them being called *Mazamorra*, the other *A–canto–de–flores* (Beside-the-flowers).

A-canto-de-flores.

Both owed their names to the words they employed in soliciting buyers: the former used to cry: ¡ *Vaya de á mil!* (Come, buy
a ticket of a thousand!) *Mil pesos de suave!* (A thousand piastres for
nothing!) ¡ *Suave como mazamorra!* (As delicious as *mazamorra!*)
¿ *Quien quiere mil pesos?* (Who wants a thousand piastres?)

The latter, a person of mean exterior, but witty and fluent of
speech, had in his young days sung couplets on the stage; he would
relate stories and anecdotes to the persons who called him in. He
was doubtless the *suertero* (ticket-seller) who sold most tickets. His
ditties were very diversified, but nearly always in this style:

> ¡ Vaya un numerito
> En un jardin!
> Una de á quinientos
> Y otra de á mil !

> ¡ Vaya un numerito
> A canto de flores!
> Hombre con mil pesos,
> Muger con amores !

> Las suertes con la verdad,
> Y la verdad con las suertes;
> ¿Quíen compra el treinta y tres mil?
> ¿ Quien quiere mil pesos fuertes (1) ?

The directors of the Beneficencia used to sell the privilege of the
lottery by public auction, and it sometimes fetched as much as
45,000 piastres yearly. The purchaser engaged to give prizes for the

(1) Come buy a little number
   In a garden!
  One of five hundred,
   The other of a thousand !

  Come buy a little number
   Beside the flowers!
  Man with a thousand piastres,
   Woman with love!

  The prizes with the truth,
   And the truth with the prizes;
  ¿Who will buy number thirty-three thousand?
   ¿Who wants a thousand good piastres?

first twenty numbers drawn, the highest being a thousand, and the lowest fifty-five piastres.

It happened not unfrequently that the lottery contractors so managed matters as to secure the great majority of the prizes for themselves, leaving little or nothing for the poor simpletons who had half-starved themselves to save the means of buying tickets. These abuses and others besides at last induced the Beneficencia to keep the lottery in its own hands, and thus give the public a certainty of fair-play.

A *suertero* (ticket-seller) of the present day.

The lottery is now drawn every month. The tickets are four reales each and the highest prize is four thousand piastres.

FACTS WHICH SHOW IMPERFECT CIVILIZATION.

The want of a good police in the capital, and other causes which space will not allow us to enumerate, give no little annoyance to the inhabitants. We will however only notice the following inconveniences :

1. The liberty left to the populace of carrying large burdens on the foot-pavement, and of thus pushing ladies and gentlemen into the gutters.

2. The being run against by a man carrying candles, fish, or

other similar articles, and having one's coat soiled so as defy all cleaning.

3. Allowing asses laden with hay, bricks, or earth, to gallop along the streets, knocking down old people and children who are unable to get out of their way.

4. The being stopped by the following courteous speech : *Dispense Vd. Caballero—permítame Vd. su fuego* (Excuse me for taking the liberty of asking for a light); *Deme Vd. su candelita* (please to lend me your cigar), and to be detained some twenty minutes while the gentleman lights his cigar by yours. This annoyance ought not to be tolerated now lucifer matches are so common and so cheap.

5. The never being able to meet any obliging person to point out a house or person you may want to find.

6. The permitting shopkeepers to obstruct the foot-pavement with goods and packing-cases, so that passengers are obliged to walk along the carriage way.

7. Making an appointment for one o'clock and having to wait till three.

8. Stealing letters at the post-office.

9. Attacking debtors in the public newspapers.

10. Passing *noches buenas* (happy nights) instead of *buenas noches* (quiet nights).

11. Sending a man to prison because he is accused of some crime, and releasing him a year afterwards, declaring him IN-NOCENT.

12. Allowing servants at hotels or coffee-houses to keep customers waiting for a beef-steak or a cup of chocolate long enough to get through three chaplets and eight litanies.

The inhabitants of the capital of Peru are exposed to all the above nuisances and many others we might mention.

BEGGARS.

The laws of Peru forbid begging and vagrancy. As a proof of the manner in which these laws are enforced, we may observe that

White beggar.

Negro beggar.

there are plenty of beggars, white, black, and yellow — indeed, of all the tints to be seen among the multicoloured inhabitants of Lima.

THE ARCADES.

Among the usages of Lima of which we regret the loss, must be counted that of walking under the Arcades on festival days. No long time since, the Sunday was divided as follows: mass at eight in the morning; at nine, breakfast; afterwards people dressed to receive

Misturera (flower-girl) of the Arcades.

or pay visits or to walk under the Arcades. They dined at three; and then went either to the promenade of the Acho or of the Descalzos, according to the season, or else received visitors at home. After dark, they went to the theatre, the church, or balls.

About one in the afternoon the Arcades became crowded with

all the most beautiful and most fashionable *señoritas* of Lima, who went thither to buy flowers and *misturas* (1).

The Arcades were occupied by flower-girls and dealers in perfumery and haberdashery. Here the newest fashions were displayed by both gentlemen and ladies. The lover was sure to find the object of his vows, and, of course, could not do less than offer her a *mistura*. The friend of a family, or he who wished to be so, there found an opportunity of showing his generosity. A dashing *caballero*, as he passed by a flower-stall before which a lady friend was standing, would coolly throw down a gold *onza*, saying to the *florista : Paguese Vd.* (Pay yourself), and walk on without waiting for change.

Among the gentlemen and ladies nothing was heard but such phrases as : *Vea Vd. lo que lleva á gusto* (Choose what you please); *¡ Gracias, caballero!* (Thank you, sir); *Señora, ¿en que se fijan esos lindos ojos?* (Madam, by what are your beautiful eyes attracted?) and other gallant expressions which no one thinks of using now. As the place was frequented by all sorts of persons, the *misturera* was for some of them a convenient intermediary, and her stall the rendezvous of many a loving couple who did not enjoy complete liberty.

(1) A nosegay of small and very fragrant flowers contained in a paper envelope

CONTENTS.

—

PART II.

PLACES OF WORSHIP.

PART III.

GOVERNMENT OFFICES AND PUBLIC ESTABLISHMENTS.

224   CONTENTS.

Paris : Printed by A. Lainé and J. Havard, 19, rue des Saints-Pères.